Lisa

Tides of the Heart

Tides of the Heart

Thomas M. Sheehan

DOWN EAST BOOKS
Camden, Maine

Text copyright ©1998 by Thomas M. Sheehan
Jacket illustration © 1998 by Jim Sollers
ISBN 0-89272-431-5 (hardcover)

Printed and bound at Thomson-Shore. Inc.

2 4 6 8 9 7 5 3 1

Down East Books
P.O. Box 679, Camden, Maine 04843
Book Orders: 1-800-766-1670

Library of Congress Cataloging-in-Publication Data

Sheehan, Thomas M. (Thomas Martin), 1926-
    Tides of the heart / by Thomas M. Sheehan.
        p.   cm.
    ISBN 0-89272-431-5 (hardcover)
    I. Title.
PS3569.H39236T5   1998
813'.54–dc21
                                        97-48923
                                        CIP

This novel is dedicated to Charlene Brusso, Dick Lynch, Virginia Palmer, Dawn Ramage, and Mary Welch. They are all members of the Tuesday afternoon writing group who helped me to successfully complete this book. Without their encouragement, inspiration, and suggestions, the novel would still be a jumble in my mind.

It is also dedicated to my wife, Lillian, who became a part-time widow while I locked myself in a room for hours at a time to write it.

Somewhere deep in that ocean vastness known as the Gulf of Maine, small fish called alewives were shoaling. Soon they would be moving into the estuaries, and sometime in April or early May, when the water reached the correct temperature, they would ascend into freshwater streams and rivers to complete their ritual of procreation.

At the same time that the alewives were shoaling on this late February morning in 1966, the sun rose in a kaleidoscope of color from a fog bank that, moments before, had blanketed a certain Massachusetts estuary with total grayness.

Watching the sunrise from the bedroom window of her classic Federal home was Miss Worthley, a wealthy, elderly, sometimes selfish, spinster. Her numerous eccentricities were often the topic of conversation among many of the residents of the nearby town of Staddleford. For example, she had never held a tennis racquet, yet she usually wore white tennis sneakers on her morning walks. This practice earned her the nickname of "Sneakers Worthley" among a few of the "townies," the term she used for some of the residents of Staddleford.

A transplanted Bostonian, she cared not one iota what

the townies called her or thought of her. She was a Worthley, a Boston Worthley, and as her late father had reminded her until the day he died, the Worthleys were a cut above the rest. Because of Miss Worthley's imperious demeanor, she had few friends in Staddleford, or anywhere else for that matter. Her only real confidant was her gardener and handyman, Flint Fletcher. Her cousin Rowena, who lived in Boston on Commonwealth Avenue, visited occasionally, and once a year, in April, Miss Worthley visited her.

The reason Miss Worthley went to Boston in April was purely selfish. When the big white star magnolia in front of Rowena's brownstone was in full bloom, the alewives would start their ascent of Staddleford Creek. Their arrival not only heralded the coming of spring, it was in itself the most significant event of the year for Miss Worthley.

She could have telephoned Rowena about the tree, but she never thought her cousin could tell if its flowers were at their peak by Worthley standards. So she would ride the train into Boston, then take a cab from North Station to Rowena's. Even before Miss Worthley rang the doorbell, she'd reach out and gently finger one of the tree's delicate blossoms. Then, and only then, would she decide if the alewives might be arriving in Staddleford Creek perhaps as soon as the next high tide, or at least within a day or two.

The two cousins would have tea together, then Miss Worthley would walk across the Public Garden and through the Boston Common to the Provident Institution for Savings. There she would meet briefly with the trust officer who managed her investments. He'd call a cab for her for the short ride back to North Station, and she'd be home in Staddleford before dark.

Miss Worthley viewed the alewives from a gazebo that Flint had built a few years earlier on Red Cedar Point, a huge out-

2

cropping of pink granite at the edge of Staddleford Creek. Here, in complete comfort, she could watch the alewives ascend. Over the years, large pieces of the granite had fallen into this section of the creek, making the water shallower than in most places along its course. As a result, the dorsal fins of the alewives were often actually out of the water as the fish struggled over the obstacles.

Occasionally, a fish would slither laterally and display its iridescent sides in shades of green and violet. Sometimes, when their flanks flashed in the spring sunshine, Miss Worthley would describe them as "not unlike the finest sterling, but more like polished pewter."

From her window Miss Worthley watched as the remnants of the fog dissipated and the sun peeked above the trees on the far side of the salt marsh. Yet in spite of the promising morning, she was pensive. In a telephone conversation with Rowena a few days before, she told her cousin that she hadn't been feeling quite right in recent weeks. Actually, the symptoms she'd been having would have sent anyone else racing to a physician. But she was a Worthley, and the Worthleys didn't patronize the medical profession for what might be just a little indigestion. Miss Worthley would not let whatever was wrong prevent her from watching the alewives ascend Staddleford Creek at least one more year. Besides, she was feeling fine that morning.

But then she reminded herself that she was in her seventies, wouldn't live forever, and in all probability would die a lonely old woman. Suddenly, she remembered the circumstances that preceded her father's death thirty years before. For weeks he hadn't been feeling well. After examining him, the family physician suggested that Mr. Worthley sell the business in Boston and retire so he could enjoy country life and the friendly, small-town people of Staddleford on a full-time basis.

"They're not my kind of people," he had snapped. "They're farmers, clam diggers, without much culture. I moved to Staddleford to get away from people after a day's work. The business is my life."

The doctor had shrugged his shoulders. "At least cut back your trips to Boston to a couple of days a week," he'd advised.

"I'll think about it," her father had said.

He'd eventually taken the physician's advice and gone to Boston only three times a week. He still didn't feel any better, and he became quite cantankerous. To get away from him, Miss Worthley went to Rowena's for a few days, leaving her father alone in the house in Staddleford. One morning the mailman became suspicious when he found the previous day's mail still in the box. He knocked; when there was no answer he tried the door, which was unlocked. He found Mr. Worthley dead in a living room chair, a copy of the *Wall Street Journal* on his lap.

Miss Worthley heard Flint's car as he drove up to the carriage house. She sighed. *I've been exactly like my father, only more so,* she thought to herself. *At least he had business friends. Flint and Rowena are my sole connections with the outside world. Maybe I should become more gregarious.*

Still enchanted by the glory of the sunrise, she glanced out the window once more, then made a decision. She vowed she would join the human race. Always one to avoid clichés, she could not think of another phrase that would describe her resolution more thoroughly. "I'm joining the human race," she said out loud. "I'm . . . I'm losing my *Worthleyness.*" She laughed at the word she had just fabricated.

She dressed and had breakfast, greeted Flint enthusiastically when he came to the door, then tidied up the house, a task she hated. Later in the morning she headed out for her daily walk, a pair of binoculars around her neck.

The temperature had risen well above freezing for the first time in two weeks. Meltwater from the snowbanks along

Staddleford Road gushed into the creek through a crudely constructed culvert.

During a storm several days earlier, the force of the wind and tide had swept huge chunks of river ice onto the salt marsh. Many of the pieces were perched precariously on the edge of the creek, empty now at low tide. As the rising temperature caused them to settle, some fell unceremoniously into the creek.

William F. Ryan, a charming, good-looking encyclopedia salesman in his middle twenties, stood on the bridge over Staddleford Creek and basked in the bright sunshine of this warm late-winter day. He had dubbed the chunks of river ice on the edge of the creek "the frozen sentinels of the salt marsh." Although he was holding a sandwich, he was so taken by the panorama before him that he hadn't taken a bite.

William's prestigious employer had assigned him to the towns on the North Shore of Massachusetts. His sales success was immediate in the affluent communities of Pride's Crossing, Beverly Farms, Manchester-by-the-Sea, Magnolia, Hamilton, and Wenham. Not known to him that morning was that he was soon to be named sales manager in a choice territory near New Haven, Connecticut.

Because it was Friday, it would have been unproductive to have scheduled afternoon appointments in Pride's Crossing or any of the adjacent towns as almost everyone would be in Boston at Symphony. William's sales manager had instead sent him to the "frontier," as he referred to Staddleford. A Miss Worthley would be there to greet William and test his salesmanship.

At that moment, Miss Worthley, returning from her walk, passed William on the bridge and snapped out an order that completely startled him.

"Don't throw your lunch wrappers into my creek, young

5

man," she said. "There's enough trash in it already." She looked straight ahead as she spoke.

William turned, but before he could collect his wits she was past him, striding up the slope at a fast clip. She was small, thin, sapling straight, and she wore beige slacks and soiled tennis sneakers. Her dark jacket was wide open and flapped like a flag in the wind, revealing her binoculars. He watched her disappear over the crest of the road not knowing, or even considering, that she might be his next potential sale.

William bit into his sandwich, his enjoyment of the scenery before him shattered by Miss Worthley's interruption. To make matters worse, his sandwich wrapper blew into the creek. Feeling guilty, he looked up the road to see if she was watching, but she wasn't. He finished his lunch and brushed himself off. It was one o'clock when he got into his car and started to drive the short distance to the next house, which happened to be Miss Worthley's.

The house was on a knoll and set back about two hundred feet from the road. A crescent-shaped driveway led to a small parking area between the main house and what Miss Worthley called the "carriage house." Flint, who was taking a breather after having leveled some of the snowbanks, was leaning on a snow shovel as William stepped out of his car and introduced himself. Flint directed him to the front door and said he'd tell Miss Worthley that she had a visitor.

In a few moments Miss Worthley opened the door. She looked at William's shoes, then at his face. "Oh, it's you. So, you're selling encyclopedias. Wipe your feet and come in."

Recognizing her voice from their earlier encounter, William did as he was ordered. Then he introduced himself and handed her his card. "I'm William Ryan. I believe we met before, down at the bridge."

"So we have," she replied curtly. "Well, with a name like that, I suppose you're Catholic."

"With a name like that, I suppose I am," he said, unfazed.

Remembering her vow of only a few hours before, Miss Worthley suddenly softened. "Would you like a cup of tea, young man?"

"I'd enjoy one if it's not too much trouble for you," he replied.

"It's no trouble, and it will relax us both," she answered, surprising even herself with the sincerity in her voice. "Why don't you go into the library?" she suggested, pointing toward the room at the end of the hall. Then she disappeared through a doorway to William's left.

As soon as he entered the library, he immediately decided that Miss Worthley was not the best housekeeper. Scattered about were copies of *National Geographic, Field & Stream,* and *Outdoor Life.* The latter two magazines were the last he would have expected to find in this household.

On the bookshelves were past and current best-sellers and books on flora and fauna, wildlife and ichthyology. There was a copy of Bigelow and Schroeder's *Fishes of the Gulf of Maine,* which William later learned was the bible for marine biologists. A copy of Rachel Carson's *Silent Spring* sat on the coffee table.

Miss Worthley reappeared, carrying a silver tray that held all the necessary ingredients for "a proper tea."

"I apologize for that uncalled-for reference I made a few minutes ago," she said as she placed the tray on the coffee table, "but if there's ever been a Catholic inside this house, I've been unaware of it."

William consoled her by saying that there probably weren't too many Protestants who ever made it inside his parent's house, at least during the time they'd been living in it.

She admitted she'd been suffering from a bad case of bigotry and said today was a good day to end it.

William noted that it was the way they were brought up and that certain elements kept the Catholics and Protestants from ever getting to know one another.

He had never talked this frankly with a person so many

7

years his senior, but on this day the conversation flowed between them as if they were old friends. They talked about many things, especially the environment. Miss Worthley told William about alewives, how they spawned in her creek every spring and what they had to contend with in order to perpetuate.

So taken were they by each other that it would have been fruitless for William to remind her why he had come in the first place. In fact, he never did start his sales pitch that afternoon, and by four o'clock Miss Worthley was calling him William.

Savoring the dialogue that had passed between them, they were silent for a moment. The sun dipped below the tree line. Its last rays, somewhat filtered by the bare branches, found a window in the library and reflected off the silver tea tray onto the walls. Staddleford Creek was three-quarters full, and the river ice groaned and floundered on the incoming tide.

When William suggested that he should be leaving soon, Miss Worthley sighed. "Please tell me one more thing before you go."

"Certainly, if I know the answer," he replied.

"How does one know the meaning of the Latin in the Catholic service?" she asked in her clipped Yankee accent.

"That's easy," he said. "In the missal we use, the Latin is on the left-hand page and the English is on the right-hand page."

"Ah!" she exclaimed. "That's fascinating." They both laughed.

"William, I laugh so little that I actually hurt from laughing so much this afternoon." She looked into his eyes. "Will I ever see you again?" she asked seriously.

"I hope so. I'll call you a day or two in advance when I know I'll be in this vicinity. Chances are, it'll be another Friday afternoon."

"William, you're welcome here anytime."

As she escorted him down the hallway to the front door, Miss Worthley came close to looping her arm in his. She opened the door and shook his hand. For a moment he thought she would never let go.

She watched him walk to his car, sad that he was leaving but happier than she had been in years.

Flint Fletcher, who usually finished his chores by late afternoon and then left, today lingered until William departed. Flint was deeply suspicious of anyone who spent more than twenty minutes inside the house with Miss Worthley.

As soon as William's car disappeared from sight, Miss Worthley rushed upstairs to her bedroom, reached into a closet, and removed a photograph—obviously taken many years ago—of a young man in an army uniform. She stared at it, her heart pounding, and said quietly, "It's almost as if he's come back from the dead."

She took one more look at the photograph and replaced it in the closet. Seconds later she retrieved it and dusted it off with her sleeve. She hastily cleared a spot among the bric-a-brac on her dresser and gave it a prominent place.

Later that evening, she placed a timeworn recording of "Poor Butterfly" on an old phonograph and went through the motions of dancing and singing that sentimental song of World War I.

When William arrived home, he told his parents about an interesting woman he had met. His mother, sensing that perhaps he had found a promising mate, was momentarily ecstatic. Her hopes were quickly dashed when he told her that Miss Worthley was older than she was. William's father just laughed.

The next morning Miss Worthley was out in the carriage house bright and early to speak to Flint. "As of last Monday, your salary has been increased by five dollars a week." Before Flint could even thank her, she said, "Now, I want you to drive me into Staddleford Center."

This was a strange request from someone who hadn't gone into town more than a dozen times in the last ten years, and then mostly to attend church services on Easter Sunday.

When they were halfway there, Miss Worthley spoke up. "I'd like you to drop me off at Lester Baldwin's General Store. I want to pick up a few groceries." Ordinarily she would have given Lester her order over the telephone, and Flint would have driven over to pick it up.

As they approached the center of town, Miss Worthley placed two one-dollar bills on the dashboard. "Flint, you go into May's Coffee Shop and have a cup of coffee and a doughnut. When I come in there in a few minutes, you go up to the counter and order me white toast and coffee. The two dollars should take care of everything, including a modest tip."

By now, Flint's easygoing manner had been altered. As he pulled up in front of Lester's, he forgot to shift into a lower gear and jerked the car like a new driver. Miss Worthley didn't seem to notice; she bounced out of the car like a schoolgirl and headed toward the store.

At nine o'clock on a Saturday morning, Staddleford Center was bustling. Miss Worthley was immediately greeted by the Reverend Leander Sparks, minister of the Staddleford Parish Church, who had long been cultivating the spinster for her wealth. His homily to her this morning was a reminder "of the necessity of providing vital services for our little church that God really built on that lovely knoll over there."

She didn't give him a chance to preach, saying she was in a terrible hurry but would see him on Easter Sunday, at which time she would pay her tithes.

The bell tinkled as she opened the door to Lester's. Upon seeing her, Lester, who always had a toothpick in his mouth, quickly snatched it out. The toothpick was his pacifier. Without it, he had a tough time concentrating even under ordinary circumstances. Because of Miss Worthley's surprise appearance, he had to excuse himself for a few moments to regain his composure.

Rather than wait for him to return, Miss Worthley walked about the store looking over the food items she was certain would please William on his next visit. By the time Lester returned, she had placed a bottle of white wine vinegar and a jar of maraschino cherries on the counter. She looked at him. "I hope next week when I come back, you'll have cucumbers and parsley that are fresher than these." She held them up in front of Lester as if they were contaminated. "These belong in my compost pile, not in my kitchen." Her tone of voice made Lester wince, but she wanted to make her disappointment known. She planned to make William her best cucumber sandwiches.

"All right, now," she said, "I'll put a few more items on the counter and Flint will be here in a little while to pick them up." As she placed the last items on the counter, she told Lester she was on her way to May's Coffee Shop.

Lester breathed a sigh of relief. As soon as she closed the door, he put the toothpick back in his mouth.

Meanwhile, Flint, who was sitting at a table in May's, was dreading Miss Worthley's arrival when in she came. In the moment it took for her eyes to adjust to the light and find Flint, the din in the crowded coffee shop subsided as if she was a gunslinger entering a saloon in a western movie. She went straight to Flint's table. With the aplomb of a butler, he assisted her into the chair.

They sat facing each other in silence as Miss Worthley waited patiently for him to place her order. Finally, calling Flint by his given name, she reminded him, "Finley, please order me white toast and coffee with cream on the side."

Flint was mortified as "pshaws" and foot shuffling broke the silence of the cozy coffee shop. He walked to the counter and repeated the order to May, an attractive bleached blonde.

13

In a couple of minutes the toast and coffee were ready. May brought them to the table, using her best manners in placing them before her distinguished guest. Miss Worthley asked for marmalade. Ordinarily the jar would have been put on the table, but for this occasion May scurried behind the counter, fetched a small dish, scooped out a portion, and placed it before Miss Worthley as every pair of eyes in the restaurant watched. Miss Worthley thanked her.

After she finished her coffee, Miss Worthley whispered to Flint that he could leave if he wanted to go over to Lester Baldwin's for the groceries. She would wait for him out front. Then she said, "Don't forget to pay May before you leave."

Flint did as he was told.

That afternoon Miss Worthley carried the phonograph downstairs into the library, where she played and replayed the old recording of "Poor Butterfly."

Although thoughts of William filled her mind, she also deliberated about the return of the phoebe that always built its nest next to where the stovepipe entered the chimney behind the carriage house. She knew she should be hearing it around the first week in March. Although it was another early sign of spring that prepared her for the arrival of the alewives, this year it was meeting William that gave her life new meaning.

The next afternoon when the telephone rang, she was sure it was William. In fact it was Rowena calling to ask how she was feeling. Miss Worthley didn't elaborate on her health but instead told her about William, "the encyclopedia salesman, who is such a lovely boy." She told her about William's resemblance to Warren, whose picture she had placed on her dresser.

Rowena was the only person alive who knew of Miss Worthley's romance of almost fifty years ago with the young army officer. Miss Worthley had met Warren at a cotillion in Boston in 1917. For three months, while he was stationed at one of the Boston Harbor forts, they saw each other two or three times a week. After he went overseas, they corresponded and had planned to marry. Shortly before the Armistice was signed, Warren was killed in action. When Miss Worthley stopped receiving his letters, she became concerned. She learned of his death months later after writing several letters to the army seeking his whereabouts.

She never contacted Warren's family, who lived in the Midwest, because she wasn't sure they were aware of the courtship. And she didn't want to add to the agony she was sure they were experiencing. After almost a year of grieving privately, she made herself attend a few socials, but she never became interested in any of the young men.

In addition to keeping the town house on Beacon Hill, which she hated because everything in Boston reminded her of this unhappy episode in her life, her parents purchased the house in Staddleford. She loved the closeness to nature she felt in the town's fields, marshes, and woods.

After her parents died, Miss Worthley became even more withdrawn, until in the early 1950s she became somewhat of an environmental watchdog when she observed what seemed to be the uncontrolled filling in and destruction of the local salt marshes and other wetlands. It was then that she noticed that the alewives were unable to get over the dam into Staddleford Pond every spring because the fish ladder wasn't being maintained.

"Good morning, Miss Worthley, could I interest you in a deluxe set of encyclopedias at a very special price?"

"William," she replied, "you are truly a rogue."

William was calling early Monday morning to tell Miss Worthley that he would be coming again on Friday afternoon. As soon as she finished talking with him, she went into the library, sat down on the sofa, and gathered her thoughts. She would take an unprecedented late-winter trip to Boston to visit R.H. Stearns, the lovely old department store at the corner of Tremont Street and Temple Place. She wanted something to wear that was more feminine than the old slacks and sneakers she'd worn at their first meeting. She knew that her wardrobe needed updating, but she'd never before been motivated to do it.

She made a date to meet Rowena on Wednesday. They would have lunch at the Ritz, which was only a short distance from Rowena's brownstone. If the weather was nice, they would walk to Stearns; otherwise, they would take a cab.

On Wednesday morning, as Flint was driving Miss Worthley to Staddleford Depot to get the Boston train, he said matter-of-factly, "Before we know it, ma'am, the 'saw bellies' will be runnin' up the creek."

She'd never cared for the nickname he used when referring to the alewives, but she was so enthused about going to Boston that she simply answered him with an unemotional, "Yes, it won't be very long now, Flint."

In Boston's North Station, Miss Worthley hailed a cab and directed the driver to take her to the Ritz. Rowena, always prompt, was waiting for her in the lobby. Over lunch they discussed what would be proper attire for this special occasion. They both agreed that a wool jacket and skirt would be correct; they would decide on colors when they saw the selection at Stearns.

As they walked through the Public Garden and across the Boston Common on this beautiful late-winter day, Miss Worthley had to stop for a few moments to feed two squirrels from a small bag of peanuts she carried in her handbag.

At Stearns it was decided that the skirt would be a Lindsey plaid. It was an easy decision for the two cousins because there was good Scots Clan Lindsey blood in their veins. Miss Worthley wanted a jacket of light gray flannel, but Rowena

16

interceded. "Gray is old. Get a navy blue jacket to accentuate your lovely white hair."

"Rowena," said Miss Worthley, "before I know it, you'll be calling me Snow White."

At that, the two cousins laughed like schoolgirls. After they calmed down, Miss Worthley chose a white blouse with a ruffled collar on which she'd pin her mother's huge cameo. Rather than black pumps with a one-inch heel, she selected dark brown loafers. She told Rowena that if she wore pumps, she'd probably trip and spill tea all over William. They laughed so hard that Rowena had to make an emergency trip to the ladies' room.

Miss Worthley was a perfect size ten, so no alterations were necessary to her jacket and skirt. Her purchases were boxed and a cab was called. The cousins left, with Miss Worthley carrying everything she had bought in one huge shopping bag.

The saleswomen, not expecting humor of any kind from the two spinsters, had a most enjoyable afternoon. For weeks thereafter, whenever there was a lull in the store, the mere mention of the cousins cheered them.

On the train ride back to Staddleford, Miss Worthley planned how she would entertain William on Friday. She *would* make him her dainty cucumber sandwiches. She'd go to Lester's again for fresh cucumber and parsley and thin-sliced white bread. Although she briefly considered that cucumber sandwiches might not be masculine enough for William, she finally brushed the thought aside, rationalizing that they were a correct item for afternoon tea regardless of a person's gender.

Her favorite part of the train ride between Boston and Staddleford was the last leg, between Ipswich and Staddleford Depot where the tracks ran along the edge of the salt marsh and, in places, across it. Most of the ice on the marsh had melted. Here and there, where there was open water, black ducks and mergansers had gathered in small groups to feed on plant and animal matter that only a few days before had been locked beneath this frozen expanse.

The marsh itself, although still drab and unproductive, was brightened by reflections of the fading blue sky in its creeks and puddles. A flock of red-winged blackbirds, startled by the train, lifted off the stubble of a cornfield, but the birds resettled quickly into their evening roosting place in a grove of hardwoods. As the train click-clacked into Staddleford Depot, several "swamp-robins," as Miss Worthley called robins who didn't migrate south for the winter, were perched in a tangle of grapevines and bittersweet, their breasts at that moment made even redder by the brilliant sunset.

Flint was waiting at the depot. He could not help but notice Miss Worthley's recent exuberance. Unable to contain himself any longer, he said as he drove her home, "Not bein' nosy, Miss Worthley, but what's all the hullabaloo been for lately?"

She answered him quickly. "That young man who was here last week is coming for tea on Friday afternoon."

"Oh," Flint said, not sure that that alone was reason enough for her newfound gaiety.

After bidding Flint good night, Miss Worthley went into the kitchen, prepared a small snack for herself, and carried it into the library. While eating, she played the recording of "Poor Butterfly" over and over again, and she examined and reexamined her new clothes. She went upstairs to her bedroom and tried on the blouse. She stared at herself in the mirror, then rummaged through a dresser drawer until she found her mother's cameo. After giving it a quick polishing with a tissue, she pinned it to the blouse. She went to bed early that evening, exhausted but happy.

*E*arlier in the day, Lester Baldwin, not taking any chances on getting another scolding from Miss Worthley, had made certain that his vegetable supplier provided him with the pick of the crop. Lester even went to the trouble of refrigerating the cucumbers and parsley.

When Miss Worthley walked into his store on Thursday morning, Lester went straight to the refrigerator, returned promptly, and proudly placed the cucumbers and parsley on white wrapping paper for her inspection.

"Lester, these are what I call fresh cucumbers, and the parsley looks lovely. Thank you." Then she looked him right in the eye. "Lester, have you ever thought that having a tooth-pick in your mouth while waiting on customers is a less than dignified habit for a businessman?"

Lester snatched the toothpick from his mouth and stammered, "I know it is, Miss Worthley, and I'm trying not to do it in front of my customers, but it's a habit I've had all my life. In fact, my father did it before me."

"Well," she replied, "you could try chewing gum, if you could do it quietly."

"Sounds like a good idea, Miss Worthley. I'll give it a try."

"Good," she said. "Now, just put these things in a bag for me and I'll be on my way."

Miss Worthley spent the rest of the day preparing what was literally a seminar on the history of Staddleford, just for William's benefit. She would give him a proper Worthley background of the old town. Actually she wasn't at all sure that she could carry on ordinary conversation all afternoon, and she was afraid that if the conversation lagged, William might leave early. From her library shelf she removed a copy of *A Brief History of Staddleford, Massachusetts,* blew the dust off it, then carefully thumbed through it and inserted small pieces of paper between the pages she would read or make reference to. Citing certain events in the town's history would surely prompt William to ask questions, thus she could extend the conversation well into the afternoon. She might even have time to go into more detail on the salt marsh, Staddleford Creek, and the big river in the estuary into which the creek emptied.

Just before she left the library to prepare supper, she took the copy of Bigelow and Schroeder and slipped a piece of paper into the section on the alewife. There's no need for me to panic about conversation, she said to herself. There will be lots to talk about.

Meanwhile, William made sure he briefed himself on environmental subjects, and Thursday evening he read several pages in the encyclopedia on items he thought she might bring up.

The clatter of sleet on the windows and clapboards of the old house awakened Miss Worthley early on Friday morning. Her first thought was that William might not come if the weather was bad. The sleet quickly turned to rain, however, and then a light drizzle. By midmorning it had stopped, although the day was still raw and dreary.

While Miss Worthley was having lunch, she decided to make a few tiny deviled ham sandwiches. Surely this boy would need something more to eat than thin slices of cucumber between thin slices of white bread.

After finishing that chore she went upstairs to change her clothes. She was an attractive woman, and in her new attire she looked younger than her years.

Miss Worthley was standing on the front steps when William arrived precisely at two o'clock. She didn't take her eyes off him as he walked from his car to the house. When he was within an arm's length, she reached out and looped her arm around his. "William, I'm so glad to see you again." Not used to displaying such fondness, she was speechless for a few seconds.

"Whoops, forgot to wipe my shoes," William said, breaking the silence.

Miss Worthley broke into a huge smile. "William, I'm going to give you a terrible thrashing." Without releasing her grip on his arm, she led him down the hallway into the library.

William gazed at her and commented on how lovely she looked. She beamed at him, then finally let go of his arm and told him to sit on the sofa.

William smiled. "Is it okay if I take off my coat?"

"Oh, you bring out the worst in me, William. Here, let me hang it up for you."

As he removed his coat, he took a dainty bouquet of dried flowers from his pocket and presented it to her. She just stood there silently, looking at the flowers and at William. Finally, she took an empty vase from one of the bookshelves and put the bouquet into it. She left with William's coat over her arm and promised to be back in a moment.

When she returned, she sat down on the sofa next to him, then remembered she hadn't put on the water for tea. She excused herself again and left for the kitchen.

With time to look around, William noticed that Miss Worthley had tidied up the room. Looking out through the French doors onto the sun porch, he could see the salt marsh beyond the field, directly behind the house. A stone wall separated the field from the woods. Flint was cutting up a tree that had fallen into the field, probably during one of the winter storms. William could hear the whine of the chain saw echoing across the marsh.

There was still snow in the woods and on the north side of the field. The gazebo, barely visible, was surrounded by three red cedar trees standing tall and dark against the gray sky. On the other side of the marsh were more fields and woods; in the distance, partly hidden by trees, was the steeple of the Staddleford Parish Church. On that bleak March afternoon, it seemed whiter than the melting snow.

Miss Worthley wasted no time in the kitchen. As soon as she returned, she opened up the copy of *A Brief History of Staddleford, Massachusetts*.

"William," she said, sounding almost like a schoolteacher, "I want to read you some of the highlights of Staddleford. If you have any questions, stop me and we'll have a discussion. Now . . . ," and she started reading.

"The plantation of Staddleford was founded in 1638, its name being derived from a town near Derbyshire, England, which bears the same name. It was derived from two words, *staddle*, meaning a foundation or platform upon which hay is stacked, and *ford*, a shallow place in a river or stream where it may be crossed.

"Staddleford, Massachusetts, was appropriately named, for all across the extensive salt marsh within the town are hundreds of staddles that have been used for years by farmers for stacking their salt-marsh hay. Staddleford Creek drains some of the adjacent uplands." Miss Worthley made a sweeping gesture as she qualified the description: "and all the land on both sides of my house, my fields and woods, and the land owned by my neighbors."

She continued reading. "Horse-drawn equipment was used in the haying operation, which was done at low tide. The hay was sometimes stacked on scows and floated up- or downstream at high tide to be unloaded and then transported by horse and wagon to the farmers' barns. There it was stored and fed to cattle.

"Seventy percent of the town is salt marsh. The upland now supports a few farms that are used for dairying and the production of English hay. Only two farmers presently use horses." She stopped reading and added, "They aren't using any horses now, William." Then she continued her dissertation.

"Today, gasoline-powered tractors as well as mechanical hay balers are used, thus negating the need for stacking hay on the staddles. There has been an increase in the demand for salt-marsh hay in recent years, with most of it being used for mulch because of its relatively weed-free composition."

William interrupted. "What about all the ditches that crisscross the marsh?"

"Good question," she replied. "Those were dug during the Depression in an attempt to eradicate the salt-marsh mosquito. There are miles and miles of ditches. They probably helped out the farmers by getting the water off the marshes faster. Then the farmers could keep their equipment on the marsh for longer periods between tides.

"I guess the ditches worked for a while," she said, "but during World War II there was little maintenance done to keep the water flowing through them. I think overall the ditching hurt the marsh. Then the state built a new highway, which further impeded the natural flow of the tide. When it rains, the fresh water stays on top of the marsh for too long. When I was a young woman, there seemed to be nothing but pure salt marsh everywhere. Now, the cattails and purple loosestrife have gained a foothold in the marsh, and that awful phragmite that looks so nice with its waving fronds

23

seems to have established itself in some spots." Miss Worthley sighed. "Well, I won't be around to see the results of all that," she said solemnly.

"Oh, dear," she exclaimed. "I forgot about the tea water. It probably all boiled away while I was rambling on. Excuse me, William," she said, and she scurried out of the library.

When Miss Worthley returned carrying the tea and sandwiches, she noticed that William was looking at her phonograph. "Sometime I'll play it for you, but let's relax a bit and have tea. Luckily the water didn't boil away. I think the tea is steeped enough; I don't want it to get too strong. Do you like cucumbers, William?"

"I like everything, but too much coffee gives me heartburn."

"Strange you should mention that," she said, "but lately I've had some heartburn. At least, that's what I call it. It seems like indigestion of some kind. Comes and goes. My cousin Rowena thinks I should have a checkup. I haven't been to a doctor in years. I just don't relish the thought of someone poking me and looking at me all over. I'm a very modest woman, William."

"Maybe your cousin knows of a woman physician you could go to," William suggested.

"Humph, not a chance," she replied. "I think Rowena rather enjoys going to doctors—young male doctors. She's no angel, and she has about as much modesty as Gypsy Rose Lee."

Miss Worthley laughed at her own joke, and her blue-gray eyes sparkled. Being with William made her happier than she'd been in years.

Steering the conversation back to Miss Worthley's health, William volunteered to seek the name of a well-respected female physician. He ignored Miss Worthley's protests that it would be too much trouble and said he would call her as soon as he had more information.

"William," she said, "you are a dear boy, and now, on with our tea."

24

The tray held a plate of cucumber sandwiches cut into dainty triangles; on another plate were deviled ham sandwiches in the form of pinwheels. For dessert there were dainty cupcakes, each topped with thick whipped cream and a maraschino cherry.

In between bites of sandwich and sips of tea, Miss Worthley told William about the alewives. "*Pomolobus pseudoharengus* is the Latin for alewife," she began. Then she stopped. "Isn't that a horror of a scientific name? But I actually enjoy saying it. It . . . it has a rhythm to it."

She reached for her copy of Bigelow and Schroeder and found the section she'd marked on the alewife, then she read from it at times but also gave William her own interpretation.

"It's an anadromous fish; that is, it grows to maturity in the ocean but spawns in fresh water. Each female deposits thousands of eggs when the water temperature reaches fifty-five to sixty degrees. Incubation lasts six days. By the end of summer, the young alewives will be two to four inches long and will have reached salt water. Most of them are only a foot long when fully grown and usually return to the stream where they were spawned."

She paused to catch her breath.

"It's a wonder any of them make it, considering what they have to go through," said William.

"Well," Miss Worthley replied, "if it wasn't for the fish ladder on my creek, hardly any of them would make it. I complained to the Division of Marine Fisheries about the huge numbers of alewives milling about just below Staddleford Pond because they weren't able to make it over the dam. Nothing was done, so each spring for a couple of years I had Flint stand below the dam with a net, scoop up the fish, and carry them into Staddleford Pond. Then the fish ladder was built. Now there's some funding to keep the ladder maintained, and we have a tremendous run every spring, but I have to maintain my vigil or the ladder will be vandalized or won't be kept in good repair."

Her expression showed concern. "I hate to see living
creatures denied the very right to perpetuate themselves.
Look what happened to the Atlantic salmon in the Merrimac
River. They're all gone."

Her voice cracked with indignation. "William," she said,
"this spring we'll have to take you on an expedition into the
deepest, darkest portions of Staddleford Creek. I'll show you
living things you never dreamed existed, and none of them
are more than a quarter of a mile from where we're sitting.

"It will have to be at low tide, and you can wear Flint's
Wellington boots. We'll start just below the gazebo and work
our way downstream to the big river. (She seldom used the
correct name of the large river into which Staddleford Creek
emptied. Instead she referred to it as "the big river.") The
gazebo's over there," she said, waving in the general direc-
tion of the marsh and Red Cedar Point.

"I like to inspect the creek at least once every spring at
low tide, just to see what the ravages of winter may have done
to it. I pick up any litter that's accumulated. If there's more
than I can handle, and there usually is, I have Flint do it. He
hates going into the creek, but he always finds some kind of
treasure and adds it to the collection of junk he keeps in the
carriage house. He's still talking about the case of beer he
found a couple of years ago. To this day I don't know if he
ever drank any of it."

Miss Worthley switched the subject to her appreciation of
Flint. "He's a good man and I'm lucky to have him around.
He's never let me down in all the years he's worked for me.
Don't understand why he never married. There's nothing he
can't do, whether it's repairing a leaky faucet or shingling a
roof. He's good on the tractor, too. Farms my fields for me.
It's a known fact I have the best alfalfa in Staddleford. Had
three cuttings of it last year. He cuts a little of the salt-marsh
hay; I let him sell some of it on his own, and we keep a few
bales for mulching the vegetable garden. I just love the smell
of that hay when I go inside the carriage house. It's so pun-

gent, like the smell of the ocean and the marsh all blended together."

She stopped and sighed. "Listen to me rambling on. Well, now, where were we? Oh, yes."

"The cucumber sandwiches are delicious," said William before she could continue.

"Oh, I'm so glad you like them," she replied. "You know, it's next to impossible to get fresh vegetables at this time of year, but my grocer keeps me supplied, providing I point a gun at his head." She laughed and William laughed with her. He enjoyed her sense of humor immensely.

"We'll have to go into Staddleford Center some afternoon," she said. "Have you ever been there?"

"Just once, about three weeks ago, for a quick cup of coffee. Hardly had any time to look around."

"You must have been in May's. Did she flirt with you?" Miss Worthley asked.

"Yes, as a matter of fact. But she's a little old for me, so I thought she was just being friendly. After a while I realized she was flirting. She's an attractive woman, in spite of her bleached hair. She asked me to come back sometime when I could stay longer."

"And what did you say, if I may be so nosy?"

"I told her I didn't come here very often, and chances were I'd probably never be back. Then she shook my hand and asked my name. Her last words were, 'Nice meeting you, Billy,' as she walked me to the door."

"Well!" Miss Worthley exclaimed. "You were lucky to get out of there so easily, if I can believe some of Flint's stories about her."

William laughed. "My mother tells me to watch out for blondes. She says they carry a curse and that they're apt to be a bit forward. The funny thing is that my mother was blond herself. Dad says he never had a chance, but the fact of the matter was that my mother was truly the girl next door."

William went on, "I think I'm partial to girls with dark hair, although I recently met an attractive young woman who has red hair. I'll probably never see her again."

"Where did you meet her?" Miss Worthley asked.

"Well, I really didn't meet her," he replied. "She was a secretary at a sales meeting I attended in New Haven. She kept popping in and out with messages for some of the brass. She didn't even know I was there."

"You don't know that, William," Miss Worthley said sternly. "Fate has a way of intervening. You have to take the bull by the horns. Do you know her name?"

"I'm not sure, but I think I heard someone call her Patricia."

"And when is your next sales meeting in New Haven?"

"I really don't know."

"William," she said, as if she was an expert in matters pertaining to romance, "you could have left something on the table at the last meeting, couldn't you?"

"I suppose so."

"Well, why don't you call the New Haven office and ask for her? Then ask if she found a certain something. It's a way to break the ice, William."

By now, William was blushing, but Miss Worthley made him promise her he would try to contact this Patricia, or whatever her name was.

"William, are there tea leaves in the bottom of your cup?" Miss Worthley asked as she looked into her own teacup.

"Yes, a few."

"Wouldn't you know . . . I forgot to use the tea strainer when I poured. This is a good omen, William Ryan. If I could read tea leaves, I would say that this young woman will become an important part of your life. Now," she said dramatically, "let my words sink slowly into your brain while I go into the kitchen for clean cups."

She left the room carrying the tray, the two teacups clattering on the saucers with her every step.

When she returned, William told her that he would call Patricia—he hoped that was her name—on Monday morning. He would say he'd lost his tie clasp and was certain he'd been wearing it when the meeting started.

Miss Worthley laughed. "Now you're getting the idea. Remember, all's fair in love and war."

"Well, I hope you're right," he said, not fully sharing her confidence.

"William," she said seriously, "I know I'm right because I usually am. Now, let's drink to it."

*I*n the stillness of the damp late afternoon, fog was forming. It followed the slope of the land, found the marsh, and settled there, then it stirred at the beck and call of every breeze.

Flint had finished cutting up the tree in the field. On his way back to the carriage house, he was sure he heard a phoebe and wanted to tell Miss Worthley. He knocked at her back door.

"That's probably Flint," Miss Worthley said to William. "Come into the kitchen with me so I can formally introduce you."

William followed her down the hallway, through the dining room, and into the kitchen. She opened the back door.

Flint was always a little slow in getting out the first words, so she spoke up. "Come in, Flint. I'd like you to meet William Ryan. William, this is Flint Fletcher, the man responsible for keeping my property so well maintained that the town of Staddleford sees fit to raise my taxes on it every year."

William chuckled as he and Flint shook hands. Flint stood silently with a rather blank expression on his face.

Then he said, almost mumbling, "Pleased to meet you, Mr. Ryan."

"Glad to meet you, Flint, but I'd rather have you call me Bill.

"Okay, Bill," Flint replied.

There was a pause. Finally Flint said, "Ah, Miss Worthley, think I heard a phoebe a little while ago, down by the sassafras clump. Thought you'd like to know about it."

"That's wonderful, Flint," she replied. "I just knew we'd be hearing one soon. Thanks for telling me. Now, I want to know the moment it starts building its nest near the stovepipe of the carriage house.

"By the way," she added, "I'm planning to take William on a safari into the creek some day this spring at low tide. Is it all right if he borrows your Wellingtons when we go?"

Flint looked down at William's feet, thought for a moment, then said, "Looks like we both got big feet. I think you can get into them, Bill."

"Thanks very much, Flint," William replied. "I'm looking forward to it. Miss Worthley's going to show me all the secrets you both have been enjoying there all your lives."

"Well," Flint commented, "not too many people ever go down there the way we do. They couldn't be bothered. I almost caught a striped bass with my bare hands at low tide a few years ago. He was cruisin' back an' forth in the shallows right where the creek dumps into the big river. I was standin' on the bank watchin' him. He was probably tryin' to grab some 'chogs. 'Chogs is little fellas that live in the creek an' the ditches an' the shallows in the big river. Not as long as your little finger. Miss Worthley said their real name is . . . what's the real name again, ma'am?"

"Mummichogs, Flint," she replied.

"That's it. Well, anyways, I sneaked around a bit, then crawled down the creek on my hands an' knees to where he was an' made a swipe at him. It was a mistake 'cause I grabbed him by the gill plate. Slashed my hand n' fingers up real bad. Had him right outta the water for a second. Had to be a twenty pounder."

Flint spread his arms, and with his hands about four feet apart he indicated the length of the fish.

"Miss Worthley said I wasn't concentratin' . . . that I was thinkin' of him in the fryin' pan before I figured on how I was gonna git him there. She was right. If I'd a been a mite more patient, he'd a been my supper for a week."

Then Flint said that he'd best be leaving, because he had to clean and sharpen the chain saw before he went home.

Miss Worthley shut the door behind him, then led William back into the library.

"I haven't even scratched the surface of all the things I wanted to tell you," she said. "For example, in addition to the mummichogs that Flint already mentioned, another fish lives in the creek with a real tongue twister of a name. It's called a ninespine stickleback. Say that three times in quick succession," she suggested with a smile.

William tried, but she had him laughing so hard that he couldn't repeat it more than twice without bungling it.

She was laughing, too. "Oh, William, you're the best thing that's happened to me in years."

William felt uneasy. "I bet you say that to all the young salesmen who come here."

"On the contrary," she replied sternly. "Hardly any of them get inside this house. Do you know, if it wasn't for that beautiful sunrise last Friday morning, I wouldn't have let you inside either. While I was watching the sunrise, I made a resolution, which I won't disclose to you yet. But I thought, after Flint told me you were in the driveway, that I'd let this chap, whoever he was, come in and talk. If I hadn't made that resolution, you never would have walked up my steps last Friday, and that's the truth."

"I'm glad you made that decision, too," said William

"To think I almost spoiled everything when I snapped at you on the bridge. Will you forgive me?"

"I've already forgiven you. Now, I have to ask your forgiveness for something." William paused. "I have a confession to make."

"And what is this confession, William?"

"Well, you had hardly passed me on the bridge last Friday when my sandwich wrapper blew into the creek. I was certain you were standing there watching, but luckily for me, you weren't. If you had, would we be talking here at this very moment?"

"Probably not, but I don't even want to think about what might have happened. This has been one of the best weeks of my life. I just wish I felt a little better than I do. Right now, as we're talking, I feel some indigestion. I actually feel a bit weak, and there's some pressure right here in my chest." She placed her hands over her sternum. "It usually goes away in a few minutes, but it worries me." She leaned back against the sofa and took a deep breath. "Just let me sit here and be quiet for a moment or two. It'll go away, I'm sure. It always does."

Concerned, William watched her for a minute, then just let her rest. Through the doors that led to the sun porch, he could see the lights in Staddleford Center with halos around them as they pierced the foggy twilight. "I should start home," he said finally. "I'm almost afraid to leave you alone knowing you're not feeling well, but I'll call you as soon as I arrive."

"I'm fine now," she replied "You may call if you wish, William, but if anything happens, Flint can be here in a flash."

"Let me carry everything to the kitchen for you," William said, and he reached over and picked up the tray before Miss Worthley could stop him.

"William," she said, "you're babying me. No one has babied me except my father when I was a child."

"I'm not babying you. I'm concerned. You went to a lot of trouble to entertain me today, and it may have been a lit-

34

tle too much for you. Now," he emphasized, "until I leave here in a few minutes, I'm the boss."

"William Ryan!" she exclaimed. "No one has ever talked to me that way in my entire adult life."

"Well, someone is now," he said. Then he smiled. "You have to admit we do get along pretty well for two people who are years apart in age and have known each other for only a week. I never knew my grandparents. They were either dead, or I was too young to remember them."

Miss Worthley followed William into the kitchen and sat down. "You're such a good listener, William. That's more than I am. I have a knack for blanking myself out if I don't agree with someone or if the conversation becomes boring."

She suddenly felt warm, so William helped her remove her jacket. Without it her cameo was revealed more fully. As soon as he saw it, he remarked on its beauty.

"It was my mother's," she replied. "I rarely wear it because it's so heavy. The setting is solid gold. Here, look at it closely." She removed it and handed it to him.

"It's exquisite," he said.

"More than a hundred years old," she told him.

He gave it back to her. "Miss Worthley, I don't know when I'll be able to visit you again. As things stand right now, it'll be at least a couple of weeks. A new salesman is taking over my territory, so it's my job to break him in. In this business, moving is essential if you want to advance."

She looked crestfallen, and he tried to explain further. "I've been salesman of the month for each of the last six months. It's a tough job. I have only one day off each week. That's Sunday. On Saturdays I usually do paperwork, and sometimes I'll even return for a second time to a good prospect in an attempt to wrap up a sale. I've heard rumors that I may be going to New Haven, although even if I do, it won't be until fall."

"What shall I ever do if you're gone from here?" she asked.

"You'll do fine. You're already making new friends now that you go into Staddleford more often," he replied. "I have an idea. The next time I know I'll be around here, I'll call you, and we'll go into Staddleford Center and have tea at May's. You can show me the sights. Any objections?"

"Yes, there's one. I don't like the idea of you seeing May again after the way you said she fell all over you."

"But you'll be there to keep her away from me," he said with a laugh.

"It's not funny, William. She . . . she could be trouble for you if you're not careful."

Miss Worthley paused. "William, if you go to New Haven, you'll meet that girl Patricia, won't you?"

"It's been in the back of my mind."

"You lie, William. It's been in the front of your mind. I think I read you like a book, you devil."

They both laughed. At that moment the most prized part of Miss Worthley's life was William Ryan.

"See, William," she said, "the entire spring is falling into place. Now, I want you to be here when the alewives arrive. It's not very far off. Let's see, it's early March. They'll be here in about six weeks, seven at the most."

She went on. "I usually go into Boston to see my cousin Rowena around that time in April. The magnolia trees are blossoming then. It's positively beautiful along Commonwealth Avenue."

She didn't elaborate on why she really went into Boston every April, so William had not the slightest idea that the blossoms were her indication of the alewives' arrival in Staddleford Creek.

"It's a long way off, but maybe we could all meet and have tea at the Ritz," she suggested.

"It's okay by me if I can work it out," William said. "But most importantly, we have to get you to a doctor in Boston one of these days. Finding one is my priority when I leave here today."

36

William stood. "Now that we've got everything resolved, I must be going, and I thank you for a lovely afternoon, Miss Worthley."

She brought out his coat and thanked him for the bouquet, then she took his arm as she led him to the front door. He made her promise not to stand outside on the doorstep while he walked to his car.

*L*ate the following Monday afternoon, William called to tell Miss Worthley that he had found her a woman doctor. Her office was on Commonwealth Avenue, and all Miss Worthley had to do was make an appointment. He also told her that he had called his New Haven office and actually talked to Patricia. He laughed as he told Miss Worthley that Patricia hadn't found his tie clasp but had remembered exactly where he'd sat at the meeting. She also told him that it was almost a foregone conclusion that he would be working in New Haven by the middle of October.

William told Miss Worthley he became so enchanted by Patricia during their telephone conversation that he forgot to ask her last name. He would inquire when he called Patricia again regarding the mythical tie clasp.

"What did I tell you, William?" Miss Worthley said exuberantly. "It was written in those tea leaves."

Miss Worthley didn't hesitate to call the doctor whom William suggested. Her name was Sutherland, a good Scots name; therefore, reasoned Miss Worthley, she would have to be competent. Over the telephone, Miss Worthley told Doctor Sutherland about the discomfort she was experiencing and mentioned the episode the previous Friday afternoon.

The doctor asked if she could come on Wednesday morning at half past ten. Miss Worthley said she could but that it would be a challenge to be there right on the dot. Doctor Sutherland told her not to worry if she was a few minutes late. Miss Worthley liked her right away.

When Miss Worthley hung up, she felt as though a huge weight had been lifted from her shoulders. It was stupid of me not to have done something sooner, she thought. "God love you, William," she said aloud, then she sank into the big easy chair in the library and stared at the ceiling for what seemed to be a long time. The phoebe called. *Phee-bee* . . . It called again, *phee-bee,* and once more, *phee-bee?* But Miss Worthley was asleep.

The sun was low but still above the horizon. The tide was on the ebb, and Staddleford Creek was carrying away more and more of the winter's accumulation of ice and snow. Over the dam on Staddleford Pond came the water, clean and fresh. It cascaded down the granite ledges and drenched the clumps of moss, green and glistening in the day's last sunbeam. It sluiced through the fish ladder in an orderly fashion. The boards had been removed last fall and would be, or should be, replaced soon to assist the alewives in their ascent over the dam and into the pond. The first day of spring was only two weeks away.

Flint knocked at the back door. He knocked again, louder. Miss Worthley stirred, woke up, and fumbled for the switch on the lamp next to her. Then she jumped up and scooted down the hallway, snapping on lights as she hurried into the kitchen. She had been asleep for an hour.

"Flint!" she exclaimed when she finally opened the back door. "I must have dozed off. What time is it?"

"Little after six, ma'am. I didn't see any lights on, so I wanted to make sure everything was all right before I left."

"Everything's fine, Flint. I'll see you in the morning." As an afterthought she said, "Oh, Flint, I'll need a ride to the depot on Wednesday morning. Have to catch the eight-fifty-five train to Boston. Plan on my coming back at the usual time."

"No problem, ma'am," he answered, then added, "did you hear the phoebe s'afternoon?"

"No, I didn't. I must have been talking on the telephone."

"Well," Flint said, "she was really chirpin' up a storm. Haven't seen her yet, but she's hangin' around. I'd bet money she's gonna be settin' up housekeepin' pretty soon. I'll be keepin' tabs on that little girl. 'Night, Miss Worthley."

"Good night, Flint, and thanks for the phoebe update," she replied and closed the door.

As she prepared a light supper, she mulled over having fallen asleep in the afternoon. True, from time to time she would have a catnap, but to have fallen sound asleep for more than an hour, that really bothered her.

"Nothing wrong with falling asleep," she thought aloud. "Probably good for me. Rowena says she has a little nap almost every afternoon, and she's younger than I am."

Then she remembered she hadn't taken a morning walk for almost a week. "That William has a firm grip on me. He's changing my life," she said aloud to no one. "I'll take my walk tomorrow morning," she vowed. "These kinds of activities have kept me pepped up all my life. And I might even hear the phoebe."

As Miss Worthley mulled over her doctor's appointment, she decided not to tell Rowena about it. But then she worried that she just might bump into Rowena. "Small chance," she thought aloud. "The cab will drop me off right at the doctor's. When she's finished examining me, and if it's a nice day, I'll cut through onto Newbury Street so I won't be going by Rowena's. Don't *have* to go to the Ritz for lunch. I'll go to Bailey's. Haven't been there for years. They have nice sandwiches. Might even go to Stearns again. I need a new sweater, some spring clothes. These baggy slacks . . ." She looked down at them. "I should throw them away. Flint's always looking for rags for cleaning things. But they're so comfortable."

She finished supper and left the dishes in the sink, not an unusual thing for her to do. She hated washing dishes. But now she was fidgety. Watching television never did anything for her, although at times she marveled how images and sounds could be produced so clearly. So she turned on the radio in the library, found a station that played classical music, turned the volume way down, and, without really looking, pulled a book from one of the library shelves. It was a book of poetry. She dropped onto the sofa, flipped through the pages to a poem entitled "Spring," and read it once or twice.

But she was distracted by worries about her health. Both her parents had died from heart complications. At least that was the opinion of their doctors. This knowledge was foremost in her mind, yet she was somewhat consoled by the thought that she herself was not a heavy eater, was moderate in all her activities, and was, in fact, probably in better health than most women her age.

She placed the book on the coffee table, got up from the sofa, and opened the French doors that led onto the sun porch. The night was clear and frosty. Outside on the terrace the wrought-iron furniture, faintly outlined by the half-moon, looked almost grotesque in the eerie light. Shivering on the unheated porch, she walked back into the library, slipped into her jacket, then walked through the sun porch and onto the terrace.

She stared at the sundial, trying to see if the moon was bright enough to cast a shadow from the gnomon. She leaned over to look at it more closely, but the shadow was too diffused to show precisely on any one numeral. She chuckled, saying to herself that it was "loony time" and she was only half crazy because the moon was only half full. She took a couple of deep breaths, walked back into the house, and went to bed.

The next morning, in spite of a light mist that was falling, Miss Worthley decided to go for a walk. But first, she poked her head inside the carriage house to say good morning to Flint and tell him she was leaving.

She walked the sloping road down toward the bridge, then stopped and leaned against the railing as she stared across the marsh. In the distance, about where Staddleford Creek emptied into the big river, she watched a marsh hawk soar gracefully in the breeze. She wished she had brought her binoculars. Just as she started to resume her walk, a woodcock flushed out of a thicket of gray birches and flew across the road in front of her. She was ecstatic—she knew Flint hadn't seen one yet. If he had, he would have told her.

She always liked the pronunciation of the woodcock's scientific name, *Philohela minor*. For the next few minutes she kept repeating it, *"Philohela minor, Philohela minor,"* giggling to herself and altering her gait to match the rhythm of the words as she spoke them.

Now that most of the snow was gone, she would be less apt to be splashed by passing cars. She wondered, because of her reputation, whether it was intentional some of the time. Now, with William in her life, people might have a different attitude toward her. Flint had probably said something about her new friend to his cronies down at May's. She really wasn't concerned about what they thought of her. The only thing that did concern her was becoming an invalid. She would rather be dead. The thought of a complete stranger in her house, taking her to the toilet or sliding a bedpan under her was depressing.

A pickup truck slowed down and stopped. It was Lester Baldwin returning from Lawrence with a load of produce nestled under an old quilt.

"Mornin', Miss Worthley," he said as he rolled down the window.

"Lester!" she exclaimed. "What a pleasant surprise!" This was a phrase she didn't use once every five years.

"Thought you'd like to know that I haven't had a tooth-pick in my mouth since the last time you were in the store, but now I'm hooked on gum."

They both laughed, especially Miss Worthley. Then Lester put out his hand, shook hers, and drove away.

She was flattered beyond words. The fact that he had ac-tually heeded her advice humbled her deeply. She felt good all over and started walking again, her head held high as she relished the cool mist against her face.

When she returned home and mentioned to Flint that she had seen a woodcock, he told her she had the jump on him on that account but that he had heard the phoebe again just a few minutes ago.

Miss Worthley headed for the house to prepare a huge lunch for herself. She intended to then play the recording of "Poor Butterfly," but she realized that it did not quite fit her mood. Instead, she turned the radio dial to classical music.

As she listened, she promised herself that some Friday she would go to Symphony, but not this season. She com-promised and thought she might go to a Boston Pops con-cert some evening in May or June. She could always stay at Rowena's, even though she disliked the idea of spending the night with her.

Miss Worthley's thoughts drifted and she fell asleep, but this time for only half an hour. When she awoke, she looked out onto the terrace and decided that the wrought-iron fur-niture needed painting. She walked over to the carriage house to tell Flint.

*T*he next morning Miss Worthley had stood in the driveway, waiting apprehensively for Flint to drive her to the depot. She hadn't told him why she was going to Boston.

Although Flint had been curious about her second trip there in a week, rarely did he question her on anything. Her trips to Boston were personal as far as he was concerned, and as the hired man it was not his place to ask her why she was going there again. Besides, when he asked her only a week ago about all her new activities, she told him about William's upcoming visits. That was a good enough answer for him.

Flint had great admiration for Miss Worthley, and more than once he had defended her to his cronies around Staddleford. When he'd built her gazebo on Red Cedar Point, she helped, and made suggestions that saved him much time and trouble. There weren't many women of any age who could do the physical work she could do. And when it came time for the annual inspection of Staddleford Creek, she was down in it at low tide slogging along like a clam digger. He once accused her of having webbed feet.

Flint was, in Miss Worthley's mind, the essence of something she couldn't describe. She once told Rowena that her feeling for him was somewhere "in the deep heart's core," the last five words in a Yeats poem she often recited to herself.

On the ride to the depot this morning, she had been unusually quiet, and she'd spent most of the hour-long train ride into Boston staring blankly out the window. Then she'd had a row with the cabdriver over the route he took to get to Commonwealth Avenue, and she told him when she stepped out of the cab that she hoped he'd be able to find his way back to North Station. He did not receive a tip.

Miss Worthley was only a few minutes late for her appointment. As soon as Doctor Sutherland introduced herself, Miss Worthley felt at ease. After a few questions about her health background and the ages of her parents when they died, the doctor asked Miss Worthley about the chest pains and whether any nausea accompanied them. Miss Worthley told her it was a feeling of discomfort in the vicinity of her sternum more than a feeling of nausea. How many times had these incidents occurred was the doctor's next question. Perhaps a dozen, Miss Worthley told her but said she hadn't been counting. The first one was about six months ago, after she'd helped Flint load bales of salt-marsh hay onto a trailer. The discomfort actually didn't occur until a while later, after she had eaten a light meal and had been sitting for a few minutes.

"How heavy were those bales?" asked the doctor.

"The wet ones probably weighed as much as eighty pounds, the dry ones about fifty to sixty pounds," she replied.

Doctor Sutherland smiled and shook her head.

Miss Worthley explained that she'd been helping Flint for years when he cut the salt-marsh hay, and that being on the marsh every fall was part of her life.

Doctor Sutherland took Miss Worthley's blood pressure, which was high, and listened to her heartbeat with a stethoscope for what seemed to Miss Worthley to be an awfully long while. The doctor made a few notes on a large card, then looked right at Miss Worthley and told her she appeared to be suffering from angina but an electrocardiogram would be necessary to confirm the diagnosis. She could have the EKG in Boston later that afternoon or at Anna Jacques Hospital in Newburyport in a day or two.

Hearing this, all Miss Worthley wanted to do was walk to Bailey's for lunch and go to Stearns. She had no desire to spend part of the afternoon in a doctor's office. Besides, she wasn't sure she could get in touch with Flint if she were to take a later train. Going to Rowena's was completely out of the question.

Miss Worthley would have the electrocardiogram in Newburyport. Doctor Sutherland said she would arrange everything. "Meanwhile," she told Miss Worthley, "I'm giving you a supply of nitroglycerin tablets. For the time being I don't believe you should change your lifestyle radically, although you may want to shorten your walks a bit. A nap in the afternoon wouldn't hurt, either. I don't mean to scare you, but please, no more helping out with the hay bales."

Miss Worthley's disappointment showed on her face. Not one to rely on pills, she couldn't recall ever having taken so much as an aspirin.

"Lots of people have angina and live quite normal lives," Doctor Sutherland reassured her. Then she deftly changed the subject by telling Miss Worthley that her skirt was lovely. "Is it a Lindsey plaid?" she asked.

Miss Worthley was surprised that she knew it. The doctor told her she wouldn't be much of a Scotswoman if she didn't know all the plaids.

Doctor Sutherland walked Miss Worthley to the door, gave her a little hug, and told her to call if anything bothered her or if she had any questions. Then she handed Miss Worthley a card on which both her office and home telephone numbers were printed.

Miss Worthley went out the door onto Commonwealth Avenue, then took Clarendon Street over to Newbury Street.

She was almost in a daze. Anyone watching her would have thought she was window shopping, but she was only staring in the shop windows and not really seeing anything. She was mad that something like this could be happening to her.

As she reached the entrance to the Public Garden, she noticed that all the ice was gone from the lagoon. A few mallards were cruising back and forth on the open water. Remembering the bag of peanuts in her handbag, she coaxed them near shore and started talking to them as she fed them the peanuts. Already her spirits were perking up. She realized she hadn't ridden on the swan boats since she was a child, and she vowed she would ride on them in April when the white star magnolia was in blossom.

By the time Miss Worthley reached Bailey's, she was famished. She devoured a chicken-salad sandwich, a dish of frozen pudding, and two cups of tea.

In Stearns she purchased light yellow cotton slacks, a pale blue cardigan, and a pair of white canvas sneakers. She would greet the spring with light colors, she told the salesgirl.

Lunch and the little shopping spree had further buoyed her spirits. When the cab dropped her off at North Station, she tipped the driver generously, which helped soothe her conscience for not tipping the cabdriver that morning.

There was still daylight left when Miss Worthley stepped off the train at Staddleford Depot. Flint was standing motionless in the shadows beneath the portico like one of the stanchions. As soon as he saw her, he sprang into action, took her bundles, and carried them to the car.

All the way from Boston Miss Worthley had deliberated how she would tell Flint about her health. She didn't want to tell anyone, but she felt obligated to let him know. After all, she mused, he would be taking her to the hospital in Newburyport in a day or two and would be asked to get her prescription refilled from time to time. It would be difficult to keep her condition a secret. And William would call tonight or tomorrow for a report, she was sure.

Flint hadn't driven more than half a mile when Miss Worthley asked him to avoid the bumps in the road. "I'm carrying nitroglycerin," she said. "If it goes up, we'll both be blown to smithereens."

"What do you mean, you're carryin' nitroglycerin?" he asked.

"Just what I said."

"You gotta have a permit to carry that stuff," he said, his voice echoing concern.

"In a manner of speaking I have, and I also have the wherewithal to get more," she stated almost diabolically.

Flint was silent for a few seconds as he tried to digest what she had just told him. "Miss Worthley, you're pullin' my leg," he said finally.

"Yes, I am," she replied.

"God, ma'am, you had me fooled for a second."

"Flint, have you heard about treating certain heart conditions with nitroglycerin?" she asked.

"Now that you mention it, I guess I have," Flint answered. "You got somethin' wrong with your heart?"

"Angina, Flint . . . a very mild case of angina," she lied in true Worthley fashion.

Flint was silent until they arrived at the house. But as they stood in the driveway after he'd deposited her packages in the kitchen, he said, "Miss Worthley, you got me worried."

"There's nothing to worry about, Flint. But tomorrow or the next day, I'll need a ride into Newburyport for another little test. After that, I just have to do what the doctor tells me to do.

"You know, Flint?" she continued. "Whenever I'm away from here, even for just a few hours, I'm always happy to get home. Today, that's especially true. Stay with me for a minute. I want to take a few breaths of air before I go inside."

The pungency of the salt marsh and the smell of the sea in the damp March dusk pierced their nostrils, especially Miss Worthley's. She felt as though she had to have those scents inside her body before she could set foot in the house. She removed her gloves to get the house keys from her handbag, then she reached out and took one of Flint's big hands in hers. "Flint, I don't know what I'd ever do without you."

Flint's usual silence followed her remark, but as he was getting back into the car, he said, "Don't forget, Miss Worthley, you call me if somethin' comes up."

As she closed the kitchen door, she found herself yawning. She reached for the kettle and made herself a cup of tea.

As much as she wanted to tell William about the diagnosis, she half hoped he wouldn't call. She sat down at the kitchen table and sipped her tea. Then she took the envelope with the tablets in it, poured a few on the table, and decided where she'd keep them.

"Well," she said to herself, "I'll have a few to carry with me wherever I go, keep a few in the library, and put some upstairs in my bedroom." She remembered an old pillbox that her mother carried years ago. "Like mother, like daughter," she said, chuckling.

Hopefully, she told herself, she wouldn't have many episodes of chest pains. She hadn't had one since last Friday when William had been here.

After finishing her tea, she put the tablets back into the envelope, collected her packages, and, holding the envelope in her teeth, went upstairs to her bedroom. She found her mother's pillbox, blew out the dust, and poured a few tablets into the box. This would be her portable supply that she could take on her walks or carry whenever she was outside the house. In a dresser drawer littered with assorted stationery, most of which was faded, she selected a small envelope and in large block letters printed the word *NITRO* on it. She counted out six tablets and placed them in it. These would go in the drawer of the coffee table in the library.

The remaining tablets would be left in the original envelope. As she went to place it on the night table, it fell to the floor. "Boom," she said. She picked it up and looked at it, still intrigued by the fact that its contents could bring her almost instant relief from pain. She would follow the doctor's orders to a tee, not because she was a good patient but because she wanted to avoid that pain.

She removed the new sneakers from the box and placed them on the floor next to her bed. She'd wear them around the house for the next few days until they were broken in.

As she was undressing she looked at herself in the mirror, wondering how a woman as slight as she was could have a heart condition. "Fat people have heart conditions," she said aloud, "not little whisps of things like me." She looked into the mirror once more, said "Ugh," and slipped into her nightgown.

*I*n the morning, after a surprisingly sound night's sleep, Miss Worthley got up early and put on her new sneakers. She wore them unlaced and stockingless, the way a child would.

The torment and frustration of the previous day haunted her. Think good thoughts, she told herself as she looked out one of the bedroom windows and concentrated on the serenity before her.

The tide was high and had flooded most of the salt marsh, giving it the appearance of a huge lake. The sun had just risen and was starting to reflect off the water. She raised the shades on all the windows, allowing the sunlight to brighten her room and her spirits along with it. The whistle of the first train into Staddleford Depot echoed across the fields, woods, and water, letting the world know that it had arrived at the same time as the sun.

Miss Worthley wondered where the alewives might be on this lovely morning. Perhaps, she thought, some of them were even now at the mouth of the big river, waiting for the right conditions so they could come sweeping up, silently and purposefully, to spawn. It would be their one great moment in a short life span. Others of their species would be collected in a seine, dumped into a barrel of brine, and used for lobster bait, or ground up for fish meal. Not a fitting end for them, she thought, which was why she wanted to guarantee that as many of them as possible made it into Staddleford Creek, spawned, returned to the ocean, and came back again the next year.

As she had these thoughts, she could feel the warmth of the sun's rays touching her face and was beginning to feel like the Miss Worthley of the day before yesterday, before she'd been told she was ill.

At half past ten that morning, Miss Worthley had her electrocardiogram at Anna Jacques Hospital. Later that afternoon Doctor Sutherland called to confirm her earlier diagnosis and to remind Miss Worthley to keep the nitroglycerin tablets with her at all times. Miss Worthley said she'd had no more episodes of discomfort or chest pain and that she was feeling fine.

Doctor Sutherland said that that was good news and told her not to worry. What she didn't tell her was that, based on the EKG, she predicted that Miss Worthley would not live more than a few months, a year at best.

Miss Worthley went for a walk. She was feeling wonderful and considered walking all the way into Staddleford Center. She decided against it, but she did walk as far as the bridge over the big river, a distance of about a mile.

The way back was uphill for about half a mile, a walk she hadn't taken since early winter. By the time she reached the crest of the hill, she was completely out of breath. As she sat resting on a stone wall next to the road, she began sweating profusely and felt an excruciating pain in her chest. Unable to even sit up straight, she bent over with her arms across her chest. She managed to get a pill out of the pillbox and under her tongue. In a matter of moments, the pain went away.

She was more stunned than anything, but she was also exhausted. If someone came by at that moment, she would flag them down, put away her pride, and ask them to take her home or tell Flint to come for her. She actually said a prayer.

It was answered almost immediately by, of all people, the Reverend Leander Sparks, who happened to be driving by. She stood up and told him she was simply enjoying the beauty of the afternoon, to which he replied in a worshipful tone: "Man who is closest to the land is closest to the Lord." He offered her a ride home without her having to ask him.

Although under normal circumstances she would have invited him in for tea, today she quickly let herself out of the car as soon as it stopped in her driveway, and she thanked him before he could say a word.

She went inside and stretched out on the sofa in the library. Even though it was still daylight, she snapped on lights in the kitchen and the library so that Flint's curiosity would not have him come knocking at the door of a darkened house in the likely event she would fall asleep. She really wanted to tell him what had happened, but she had told him enough already and didn't want to needlessly alarm him. In a matter of moments, she was asleep.

The telephone rang at least five times before she awakened. It was William calling for a report on her examination. She was happy to hear from him and, more importantly, have a shoulder to lean on. He thought she sounded disconsolate as she gave him all the details of her visit to Doctor Sutherland, the EKG, and her frightening experience that afternoon. She told him that although it was difficult to like someone who gave you bad news, she thought she would come to like Doctor Sutherland even more than she did already.

Then William told Miss Worthley his latest news. He had actually met Patricia the previous day at a hastily convened meeting in New Haven, a portion of which was taken up by the announcement naming him sales manager. In the few minutes he had to speak to Patricia alone, he admitted to her that the lost tie clasp was a ruse to give him a chance to introduce himself. Patricia told him that she had been sure it was but went along with the story anyway.

Hearing that made Miss Worthley forget her troubles. "See, William, my prediction is coming true," and they both laughed.

William told her he'd be near Staddleford on Friday and would drop by and take her to Staddleford Center, where she could show him all the points of interest. "We'll walk slowly," he promised. "Then we'll top off the afternoon by having tea at May's."

As soon as Miss Worthley finished speaking with William, she played the recording of "Poor Butterfly." She had stepped into her new sneakers and in her reverie went through the motions of dancing and singing, the whole time half tripping on the untied laces.

When William arrived at Miss Worthley's on Friday afternoon, the first thing he said was, "Don't forget your tablets."

She told him she was turning into a hypochondriac—envelopes full of tablets scattered all over the house and constantly taking her own pulse trying to determine if it was too slow, too fast, or had stopped completely. "The day it stops, I'll never know it," she said, laughing.

It was a cold, blustery March afternoon, and after they had strolled along both sides of the short main street in Staddleford Center, Miss Worthley led William up the knoll to the Staddleford Parish Church. She told him that, years before, she had gone into the belfry with the deacon and that from there the view was spectacular—probably the best view of the marsh in all of Staddleford. She told William that if he looked carefully through the tops of the trees, he would be able to see her house. It was a view that always intrigued her.

It was her view through the other side of the mirror—her "Alice through the looking glass" view.

"I suppose you think I'm crazy when I confide in you this way, William."

"On the contrary. I envy you for having such a vivid imagination."

After she and William left the church, they headed back down the knoll and walked slowly over to May's Coffee Shop. Ever since William had stopped there for coffee a few weeks before, May's penchant for handsome young men had been activated. She hadn't forgotten him, and she'd been hoping that he'd drop in again. She recognized William instantly and, in a sultry voice, said, "Billy, you've come back to me." Then she saw Miss Worthley and asked in a puzzled tone, "Are you together?"

"We are," Miss Worthley replied in a voice as chilly as the March wind. "William is my escort, and as soon as you see fit to seat us, may we please have a menu?"

An eye-for-an-eye exchange took place between the two women, with Miss Worthley winning the first round.

Somewhat taken aback, May took a menu off the counter and placed it on a table directly in front of her. William, ever the perfect gentleman, helped Miss Worthley into a chair and then sat down himself. He was facing the counter. Already, May was giving him her most seductive smile.

Miss Worthley noticed the expression on William's face as a result of May's attention. "William, I'm getting a little glare from the sun shining through the front window," she said. "It will get worse as the sun sinks lower. Let's move to another table."

It was near closing time, and May had just finished mopping the floor. All the chairs were on the tops of all the tables except the one where they were sitting.

"I think May would rather we stay where we are," said William as he looked around the empty restaurant.

"William," Miss Worthley said in a loud voice, "we're

moving to another table." She got up and walked over to a table next to the wall. "William, help me remove these two chairs." Then she looked at May and said sweetly, "May, dear, the sun is in my eyes. You don't mind if we move over here, do you?"

May rolled her eyes and said sarcastically, "Not as long as your handsome escort takes down the chairs for you."

"Well, thank you, May. You're very kind."

Miss Worthley looked at William, who was still seated and looked quite embarrassed over the whole episode. "William, please take down these chairs."

This time, when Miss Worthley sat down, she made sure she was facing the counter and William's back was to it. "There," she said to May, who had marched over to their new table, "that's better, much better. Now, I think I'll have an English muffin, well done, with marmalade. I haven't had an English muffin in years."

"I'll have the same, and we'll both have tea," William said.

"May," Miss Worthley asked, "could we possibly have our tea in a pot, if it's not too much trouble?"

"Ordinarily we don't serve it in a pot, but since this seems to be a special occasion, we'll make an exception," May replied with a touch of irony in her voice.

"That will be lovely," Miss Worthley said.

As May prepared their orders, she wondered about the relationship between these two. She looked at Miss Worthley from behind the counter and asked bluntly, "You two old friends or somethin'?"

"I'm William's great-aunt on his mother's side," Miss Worthley replied matter-of-factly.

"Oh," said May, quietly accepting Miss Worthley's reply as the truth.

William had to look away for a moment to keep from laughing.

Then Miss Worthley quickly added, "William's reason for visiting is to let me know of his forthcoming engagement to a lovely young lady from New Haven. So you see, this *is* a rather special occasion for us."

"Well, congratulations, Billy," May said. "I have to say she's a very lucky girl."

"She certainly is," Miss Worthley said. "And do you know, May, she has the loveliest *natural* red hair a woman could possibly have, plus the personality to go with it. So William is a lucky boy, too."

Having just seen and heard Miss Worthley at her best, William was having difficulty maintaining his composure.

When he walked to the counter to pay the check, May leaned over and whispered, "Come back again, Billy—without 'Auntie.' I'm here every day except Sunday, and it's a hell of a lot closer than New Haven."

A late March storm mocked the arrival of the vernal equinox by blanketing the countryside with eight inches of wet snow. But a brief warm spell followed and removed every trace of it.

Flocks of red-winged blackbirds descended on the field behind Miss Worthley's house almost daily, and she finally heard the phoebe. The slow greening process of a New England spring was taking place.

In early April the primroses next to the driveway were budding. One warm afternoon Miss Worthley potted up a clump of them and brought them indoors. They were a gift for William's mother.

The crocuses and early tulips were flowering, and the purple blossoms on the azalea next to the sun porch danced in the wind. Migrant robins, not the swamp variety that wintered in Staddleford, had arrived the previous week and were common now. One had taken up residence in a hemlock tree near the house, and every evening at sunset its melodious warble marked the end of another April day.

Flint reported to Miss Worthley that on a flounder fishing trip near the mouth of the big river, he was sure he had seen alewives breaking the surface. She would have to call

Rowena for a report on the status of the star magnolia in front of her brownstone. *"Magnolia stelatta,"* she said, then repeated the flowering tree's Latin name again, enchanted by the image of the tree itself as well as its celestial-sounding name. She repeated it once more.

Normally she would know almost to the day when the tree would be in full bloom, but the weather this year had been unpredictable. She didn't want to go to Boston just to check on the tree; she was fearful of having an angina attack on the train or while she was walking alone in the city.

She'd had only one incident of chest pain since the one at the top of the knoll a few weeks ago, and once again the tablet had brought her quick relief. Nevertheless, she was trying to be more cautious, walking only as far as the bridge over Staddleford Creek and taking a nap almost every afternoon. She was itching to get into the creek at low tide for the annual inspection, but she wanted William to come along. He hadn't called in more than a week, and she hadn't seen him since the afternoon they'd had tea at May's. Miss Worthley knew that he was busy breaking in his successor and was spending most of his time with the man.

One noontime, she was in her library reading a copy of John Marquand's *Timothy Dexter Revisited.* She had just closed the book and marked her place with a single flower taken from the dried bouquet William had given her on his second visit.

She was feeling restless and wanted to do something. Although she didn't have the stamina she'd had less than a year ago, she thought she could at least sit on the terrace in the warm sunshine. Once outside, however, she was too fidgety to sit for more than a moment. Instead, she filled the birdbath and found a broom to sweep away some of winter's debris from the flagstones. She sat again, looked toward the gazebo, then stood up and, with the broom over her shoulder, walked down the path to it.

The dampness had swollen the gazebo's wooden door,

and she had difficulty opening it. Inside, there were shells of acorns and hickory nuts scattered about the floor by squirrels who had made their winter residence here. She swept these out the door. The day was warm enough to have activated some wasps that had been hibernating inside the gazebo, and they were bouncing off the inside of the screens. She left the door open, hoping they would leave. "I'm giving you three minutes to vacate the premises," she warned. "At the end of that period, I expect you all to be gone, or else I shall take sterner measures." She swiped at one of them with the broom as if to demonstrate her threat.

She walked a few steps to the edge of the pink granite ledge and looked down at the water. There weren't many places lovelier than Staddleford Creek at noontime on a sunny April day. The incoming tide gurgled and cooed softly like a contented baby. Clumps of thatch and salt-marsh hay and pieces of rockweed swept by. A mussel shell bobbing on the surface was caught in the vortex of a tiny whirlpool and gyrated dizzily until it was sucked beneath the turbid water. The only thing missing was the alewives. She would simply have to check the blossoms on the star magnolia herself. She walked up to the carriage house and told Flint she would be taking the train into Boston the next day. So much for her resolve to call Rowena instead of risking another trip to the city.

The next morning while Flint was driving her to the depot, he said casually, "I'm watchin' out for the bumps, ma'am," and they both laughed. Then he said, "Hope you got some of them with you."

"I have, Flint, and thanks for your concern," she replied.

On the train, her mood was much better than on her previous trip. She could hardly remember that ride into Boston when she went to see Doctor Sutherland. Now, almost a month later, spring had arrived. Every time the train raced past a clump of daffodils or a forsythia bush, she craned her neck until they disappeared. By the time the train rolled into North Station, she had a sore neck.

She told the cabdriver to go down Commonwealth Avenue from Massachusetts Avenue so she could see every lavender-colored magnolia on her way to Rowena's. The white star magnolia was visible long before the cab reached it.

"Stop at that beautiful tree with the white blossoms on it," she told the driver. "I'll get out right there."

She stood on the edge of the sidewalk near the street, looking at the tree as if it were a shrine. Then she walked over to it, reached out, and touched the petals ever so lightly. She concluded at that moment that the tree was in full bloom. While she was trying to remember the time of the next high tide, she heard tapping from a window in the brownstone. It was Rowena. Miss Worthley waved back in acknowledgment.

Rowena opened the door. "Well, aren't you the gadabout? The last time we talked on the telephone, you didn't say anything about coming here today. But I suppose I should have known."

"I meant to call, but then I thought I'd surprise you," Miss Worthley said.

"Well, you did, completely. Come in, come in, dear," Rowena told her.

The two cousins sat down facing each other. "My, you look a little pale, cousin," Rowena said to Miss Worthley.

"Well, Rowena, I have lots to tell you."

"Yes?"

"Ah, er . . . I went to see a doctor recently."

"You've never done that!" Rowena exclaimed. "Well, let me hear all about it."

If there was one person in the world who thrived on the details of a physical examination, it was Rowena. She had no ailments herself, except the ones she manufactured. After having read that the appendix is located about three inches to the right of and slightly below the navel, she described her condition to the doctor as "those recurring pains like appendicitis." Therefore, a doctor examining her for this possibility would start probing near that part of her anatomy.

64

Rowena still thrived on the memory and excitement of those many examinations for a medical problem that didn't exist.

"Anyway," Miss Worthley said to Rowena, "I thought I might have some kind of indigestion, but it turned out that I have angina. And now after three or four weeks, I just don't feel the way I think I should. I'm convinced that once a doctor says there's something wrong with you, psychologically you feel worse. She told me to take one of these tablets whenever I have a chest pain." Miss Worthley held out the pillbox for Rowena to see. "And, I must tell you, I had one frightening episode a few weeks ago while out walking."

Rowena interrupted. "Did you say '*she*?'"

"I did," Miss Worthley said. "I went to a woman physician. You know how I hate being examined by a doctor. William told me she was highly recommended. You'd like her, Rowena. She has a good Scots name—Sutherland. She's just up the street from here."

"I would never consider going to a female physician, cousin. You should know that," Rowena said. The two women giggled.

"You're a naughty girl for not dropping in to see me on that trip," Rowena added.

"I intended to, but once Doctor Sutherland said I had angina, all I wanted to do was get away and go hide somewhere."

"You poor thing."

"Don't pity me, Rowena. Lots of people have angina and live with it, and that's exactly what I'm going to do. I feel fine today and I want to go for a ride on a swan boat. Will you come with me?"

"You're going to be disappointed," Rowena answered. "The boats don't start until the nineteenth of April."

"Oh, dear," Miss Worthley said, her spirits somewhat dampened.

"Well, at least let's get out of this stuffy old house and go for a walk on this beautiful day," Rowena suggested. "We'll find a bench in the Public Garden in bright sunshine and get some color on that pale face of yours."

When they reached the sidewalk, Miss Worthley stopped for a second look at the star magnolia. "There are at least two or three more in the Public Garden," said Rowena. "We can look at those, too."

"I know there are more, but they're not as beautiful as this one," Miss Worthley commented.

"Well, we can at least look at them. Now, let me hear much more about this William who seems to have taken up so much of your time lately."

They entered the Public Garden, found a bench in the sunshine, and sat down. As they watched the workmen apply fresh coats of paint and varnish to the swan boats, Rowena asked if William really did look like Warren, whose photograph Miss Worthley had taken out of the closet shortly after her first meeting with William.

Miss Worthley told Rowena that their hair color was a bit different but otherwise they could have been twins. In fact, she had once asked William if he had any relatives in the Midwest. He didn't.

"Oh, dear," Rowena said, "war is such a waste and so cruel. To think what might have happened between you two."

"Please don't remind me, Rowena," Miss Worthley said. "At this point in my life, I have no regrets. At least I don't think I have any. It was a long time ago, and there was no guarantee that everything would go the way I hoped it would. He could have come home and taken up with the girl next door. These things happen, Rowena. . . . But his dying did seem so . . ." She stopped talking for a moment and let out a sigh.

"Do you know, Rowena, it was years before I even wondered if Warren had died instantly or if he had gone through a great deal of pain before he died. I suppose I could have been morbid and written letters to some of the soldiers he served with in order to get all the details of his dying. But if

I had, the agony of hearing them might have been worse. I'm glad I didn't write to them."

She sighed again. "Thank God I have you and Flint, and now William, although I won't have him much longer because he's going to New Haven. But Lester Baldwin, my grocer, seems to have taken a liking to me lately. Then there's the Reverend Sparks, who will at least be there to consecrate my body before they put it in the ground."

Her voice cracked and she looked on the verge of tears. Rowena pulled her close, hugging her like a mother consoling a child. "There, there, love. You've been through a great deal lately."

One of the workmen, whose back was to them, had just put the finishing touches on one of the swan boats. He stood up, paintbrush in hand, and exclaimed to his fellow workers, "There, she's all shipshape and ready for another summer full of screamin' little bastards!"

The workmen all laughed, and so did Rowena. Miss Worthley seemed to regain her composure, and the cousins walked across Arlington Street to the Ritz for lunch.

Miss Worthley may have had her way of gauging when the alewives would arrive in the creek, but Flint Fletcher had his, too. It was called intuition.

About the same time that Rowena and Miss Worthley were being seated by the maître d' at the Ritz, Flint was standing next to the gazebo, whistling and looking down at the spot where huge pieces of granite had fallen into the creek. They formed a barrier that, depending on whether the tide was incoming or outgoing, created an eddy in the water on the upstream or the downstream side of it.

Flint heard a splash. Looking toward the downstream side of the granite, he saw at least half a dozen alewives milling about in the ripples. It was almost high tide, and the granite was covered by three to four inches of water. Suddenly, one fish sluiced across the granite, followed by another, each disappearing into the wash of the eddy on the upstream side. In half a minute, all the alewives had slipped across the granite and disappeared upstream.

Seeing the alewives return to Staddleford Creek before Miss Worthley did was nothing new to Flint, and he continued whistling. Many times in past years, he never told her he'd seen the alewives before she did. Every spring around this time, she'd ask him if he'd seen any alewives in the creek, and he'd always say she hadn't given them permission to come up yet. She'd laugh and tell him to tell them they had her permission.

As soon as Flint picked up Miss Worthley at the depot, she volunteered the information that the magnolia was in full bloom even before he had a chance to ask if it was. She wanted to know when the tide was high and he told her noontime. "I wonder if they could have started to go upstream already and I missed them. Oh, well," she added uncharacteristically, "there'll be more."

Later that evening it started to rain and turn colder. The next morning it was unseasonably cold and snow flurries fell off and on all day. At night, the temperature dropped well below freezing, even in Boston. Rowena called to report that the blossoms on all the magnolias on Commonwealth Avenue were blackened by the frost.

The cold snap also lowered the water temperature in the big river and Staddleford Creek. This meant that none of the alewives would ascend the creek until the water warmed up again.

William called Miss Worthley with the news that he had become so enamored of Patricia that he'd called his mother "Patricia" one morning at breakfast. He had been back and forth to New Haven several times and had taken Patricia to lunch three times so far. He mentioned that his visits to Staddleford to see Miss Worthley were good for his morale, and that he might just drop in unannounced some afternoon. He said he was looking forward to sitting on the sun porch or out on the terrace with her. "Some warm day this summer," he said, "I want to have a large glass of pink lemonade with you." Then he added laughingly, "You know, Miss Worthley, I still want to sell you a set of encyclopedias."

"At this point in my life, William dear, you may have to settle for the pink lemonade."

*I*n addition to celebrating the resurrection of Christ, Easter Sunday gave the Reverend Leander Sparks his best chance of the year to remind the congregation of its duty to pay tithes. Although he said he was uncomfortable asking for money, he used the phrase, "Those who pray, pay," over and over again.

Miss Worthley, like many members of the congregation, was attending her one church service of the year. She told Flint after the service that she hoped any church mice in the Staddleford Parish Church were all as well fed as the good Reverend Sparks was, that she'd memorized the Easter sermon ten years ago and could deliver it better than the Reverend Sparks could, and that the Reverend Sparks reminded her more of a harpooner in the bow of a whaleboat than a preacher in a pulpit. Flint joked that he was going to tell everyone in Staddleford what she had said.

Then Lester Baldwin came over to wish her a Happy Easter and give her a small box of candy. In spite of her sarcasm, she was overwhelmed. She tried to be inconspicuous as she dabbed her teary eyes.

Miss Worthley had been feeling especially good. She called Doctor Sutherland the day after Easter to tell her she hadn't had an angina attack for some time. The doctor explained that people don't get over angina the way they get over a cold; it was something they would always have and must live with. She told Miss Worthley that the reason she was feeling better was because she had cut back on her physical activities and was napping every afternoon. "Spring oftentimes gives people a feeling of well-being," she added.

Miss Worthley drove the last of the wasps from the gazebo on the morning of April 24, then she walked as far as the bridge over the creek. As she stood there, she had a premonition that the alewives would be coming upstream on that afternoon's high tide. After all, she reasoned, the cold spell was over, and the water would be warmer than it had been in days.

Around two o'clock she walked back to the gazebo, but instead of going inside she sat in the sunshine on a large, flat stone. The thermometer on the north side of the gazebo registered seventy-four degrees. The air was spiced with the scent of wet salt marsh and rich, loamy soil, the latter from Flint's plowing of the field behind the house late that morning. It seemed as if every robin in Staddleford had descended on the field and was feasting on the earthworms brought to the surface by the plow.

Miss Worthley had removed her sweater and was using it for a cushion. As she sat there, a male red-winged blackbird was seesawing back and forth on the frond of one of last year's reedy phragmite stalks. The bird's red epaulets added a splash of color to the still-drab salt marsh. As the bird called to the world, Miss Worthley mimicked it by reciting her interpolation of its lovely song: "O-ka-lee, Cong-quer-ree, You-choottea, O-long-tea! Gl-oogl-ee, Conk-a-tree, Quange-se-tea, Shoo-chong-tea!"

72

At that moment, she was the happiest she had been all spring. She laughed out loud, then alternately daydreamed, recited poetry, and stared at the sky. Suddenly she stopped and listened. As she looked down at the water, she saw the shadows of alewives in the ripples. They slid across the granite barriers like eels, three and four at a time, then vanished upstream.

She moved to the edge of the creek and lay down, her head actually over the ledge not ten feet from the fish. She wanted to run back to the carriage house to tell Flint, but she didn't want to chance missing a moment of the spectacle. Her heart was pounding so hard that she feared she might have another angina attack. She guessed that about a hundred alewives passed her on their way upstream.

A faint southeasterly breeze carried the sound of the church bell across the marsh. Then the wind intensified enough to shake whatever leaves still clung to the oak trees. The blue sky was now paled by haze, and the temperature started to fall. The wind made wavelets in the creek, and the red-winged blackbird stopped singing. The tide was on the ebb, and the alewives were gone for that day.

Miss Worthley put on her sweater, took one more look at the water, and half shivered, then she walked back toward the carriage house to tell Flint. She saw him with the robins in the freshly plowed field; he was competing with them for earthworms, probably so he could fish for white perch in the big river. The alewives weren't the only creatures in the estuaries on those early spring days. While she waited for Flint to return to the carriage house, she picked a few daffodils and checked on the phoebe's nesting progress near the chimney.

One afternoon in May, William dropped by for a visit. The alewives were still running upstream in abundance and, as luck would have it, the tide was high. For the first time,

William saw the alewives. As he and Miss Worthley sat in the gazebo afterward, he told her he could understand her great enthusiasm for the alewives. Seeing them made him feel humbled. Finally the blackflies, now at their worst, found their way inside the gazebo and drove William and Miss Worthley back into the house.

They were on the sun porch having tea when Miss Worthley handed him a small jewelry box. "This is for Patricia. You may open it if you wish."

William did, and inside was the cameo that had belonged to Miss Worthley's mother. He was speechless. He stood up, leaned over, and kissed Miss Worthley on the forehead.

"William Ryan," she said, "the last person who kissed me was my father, right after my mother died, and that was a long time ago. I won't wash my forehead for a month, you Galahad." She paused. "Now, there's a catch to this, William. You mustn't give it to Patricia until you're formally engaged. Is that clear?"

William laughed. "It is, but you're rushing me, Miss Worthley, you're rushing me." And they both laughed.

Then Miss Worthley turned serious. "When do you think you'll be near here again, William?"

"I really can't say," he answered. "The company is trying to get me to go to New Haven before fall, but Mother and Dad are selling the house and moving into an apartment. Dad's retiring next month, so I'd like to see them all settled before I go. I've told the company that October 15 is the earliest I can be in New Haven on a permanent basis. Patricia wishes I was already there. So do I, but I don't feel I should leave yet. The new salesman still has a lot to learn, and I don't want him half trained when I leave. He needs to be up to speed, or it could come back to haunt me."

As William was about to depart, he told Miss Worthley that she was a treasure, and he kissed her on the forehead again.

"William!" she exclaimed in a feeble attempt to be stern.

74

"If that's the method of salesmanship you use on those Pride's Crossing matriarchs, I'll never speak to you again."

He laughed and assured her it wasn't.

She remembered the primrose she had potted for his mother, and she darted out to the kitchen for it. When he saw its dazzling yellow blooms, he knew his mother would be delighted. Miss Worthley told him that after the blossoms faded, the primrose could be set in the ground and would blossom again next spring. He thanked her and kissed her on the forehead for the third time.

"You're getting too familiar with me, young man," she said as she walked him to his car.

She threw him a kiss as he drove away, then walked over to the carriage house to say hello to Flint. He told her that William's presence seemed to perk her up. William's visits *did* make her feel good, she said, for one reason in particular, but she wouldn't burden him with it at the moment.

Flint asked how Rowena was and remarked that she hadn't been out to Staddleford for some time.

"It's strange you should mention that, Flint," she said. "The last time I talked to her on the telephone, she said she might have a surprise for me. I'd almost forgotten she'd even said it. I think I'll call her right now. She's probably inherited more money. That's what it is, I'm sure.

"Oh, before I forget, Flint," she added, "when William and I were in the gazebo, there were more blackflies inside than there were outside. Do you suppose there's a small hole in one of the screens?"

"I'll walk down there right now and have a look," he replied.

"If you don't mind, wait for me down there. I shan't be too long."

*B*ack at the house, Miss Worthley was reeling from Rowena's "surprise." A doctor, a widower, who had examined her a number of times for her recurring appendicitis symptoms, had proposed to her, and she had accepted. He had taken her to dinner twice and to the opening night of the Boston Pops. After the concert, they had stopped at a cozy little restaurant on Newbury Street.

"That's where it all happened," Rowena had just told Miss Worthley, then asked her giddily, "At my age, who am I to turn down something like this?"

They would be married in June at a small ceremony and would live in Rowena's brownstone. Even though Rowena was a year or two older than Charles, she had already purchased a copy of the controversial Masters and Johnson's *Human Sexual Response.* She wanted to be prepared for any eventuality, she told her shocked cousin.

Ordinarily, Miss Worthley wouldn't discuss personal issues with Flint, but in this case she had to talk to someone. She was walking as fast as she could toward the gazebo to tell him the news when she realized she hadn't even congratulated Rowena. She also realized that she really didn't want to go to the wedding—any wedding for that matter. She hadn't been to more than four or five weddings in her entire life. And to go to this wedding unescorted would bother her even more. She decided, however, that she *would* have the couple for tea before the wedding day.

As she headed for the gazebo, the tide was well on the ebb. Five or six herring gulls squawked and fought with one another in an attempt to fill their bellies on the few alewives trapped in a shallow pool near the mouth of the creek. The salt marsh, flecked with strands of new green growth, was finally taking on a vernal look. On a wooded knoll the poplar leaves, lush and fully formed, mocked the bare oak trees and shook in the quiet breeze.

Flint was coming out of the gazebo. She started talking while she was still twenty to thirty feet from him. "Flint, the older I get, the more I realize that life is not always green pastures and still waters."

"Didn't quite hear ya, ma'am," he said.

"Oh, never mind, Flint. But do you know what Rowena's gone and done?"

"No, ma'am, I don't. But before you tell me, let's go inside here before these blackflies carry us off. I found a hole in the screen and stuffed it with a rag. Shooed most of 'em outside. Besides," he added, "your face is redder 'n a McIntosh apple in October. You better calm down a minute before you tell me anything."

She was surprised by Flint's firmness, but she followed him inside the gazebo and sat down. While they both slapped at the remaining blackflies, she told him of Rowena's engagement and forthcoming wedding and how she didn't want to attend. "Now, what do you think of a woman seventy years old getting married?"

Flint didn't answer right away. He looked at the floor, swiped at a couple of blackflies, then moved his feet. Finally he took a deep breath. "Miss Worthley, I don't see anything wrong with it. I always thought Miss Rowena was kind of a character. Every time I picked her up at the depot, she'd have me laughin' before we got out on the main road. Kinda bothered me that she always sat so close. Smelled real good, too."

He hesitated a moment. "Now I'm sayin' this kinda confidential-like, ma'am. She always gave me a little kiss on the cheek whenever she was gettin' off or on the train, providin' you weren't with us, of course. She's the type a woman probably shoulda had a man a long time ago."

He paused once more. "She reminds me a little of May, but lots more proper, if ya know what I mean."

"I know what you mean, Flint. She's always had an eye for the male body," Miss Worthley replied.

"You hit it right on the head, ma'am."

Neither of them spoke for a few moments. Then Flint said, "Miss Worthley, I think this doctor fella's a lucky man. He's found someone he cares for. There's a lot of us out there who go through life and then die without someone we love 'cause we just never told 'em the right words."

"Finley Fletcher!" she exclaimed. "You're an old softy deep down, aren't you?"

"Guess I am, ma'am," he replied. "I think you should go right back up to the house, call Miss Rowena, congratulate her, and tell her it took you a few minutes to get over the shock of hearin' the news and you can hardly wait to go to the weddin'."

She stood up. "Flint, that's exactly what I'll do. I can't thank you enough for this . . . this little tête-à-tête."

"What was that again, ma'am?" he asked.

"Our little private conversation."

"Oh, glad to help out."

"Flint," she said as she was leaving the gazebo, "we'll have to have more of these heart-to-heart talks."

"That's okay by me," he replied. "I was in a talkin' mood today anyways. Think I got a bad case of spring fever." He took off his cap and swatted a few more blackflies.

∞

As Miss Worthley walked determinedly back to the house, she decided she would invite Rowena and Charles for tea right away. She even thought of asking Flint to escort her to the wedding. She knew he would do anything she asked. Rowena would love having him, and he'd go reluctantly to please her. But it would be awkward for him, and he wouldn't enjoy himself.

What about William? No, he had enough to worry about. For an instant she thought of Lester Baldwin as an escort. No, not Lester. Then she realized that all her life she'd done almost everything alone. To go to a wedding unescorted at her age? Perfectly proper. There, it was all settled.

But she continued to stew over it just the same. It would be a long day. The train to North Station, a cab to Brookline, the train back home, then Flint meeting her at the depot at God knows what hour of the night.

"Clothes? I have to wear something dressy," she said out loud. "Get something chintzy, look like a floozy, and they'll all have something to talk about." She giggled. "No, I couldn't do that. It would break Rowena's heart."

She continued musing aloud. "I'm not shopping for clothes in Boston. There's a nice store in Newburyport. I should spend more time there anyway instead of going all the way into the city. And Newburyport is only ten minutes from here. Flint likes to go there and poke around. Thank God I have Flint."

As she picked up the telephone to call Rowena, she thought about the difference between fondness and love. There has to be a word to describe my feeling for Flint, his feeling for me. I'm almost ten years older than he is.

Down in the gazebo, Flint had taken a tape measure from his pocket and was measuring the section of the screen he'd be replacing, whistling as he did it. The water in the creek, which gurgled at least several octaves lower than his shrill whistle, was much more in harmony than his whistle with all the sounds pouring forth from a salt marsh coming to life on a spring afternoon.

When William called about a week later, Miss Worthley told him of Rowena's forthcoming marriage. He said it sounded wonderful.

"You'll have a lovely day," he added, "especially because you haven't been to a wedding for some years."

"It'll be a long day, that's for sure," she said with a sigh.

She mentioned she would be having Rowena and Charles for tea the following Sunday afternoon. "I hope Rowena won't hang all over him like a silly schoolgirl, but who knows? He may be the type who wouldn't allow such conduct. Rowena says he's very proper, and a real gentleman."

William told her that Rowena's behavior with Charles wasn't her concern, and that before the afternoon was over she would probably have a few good laughs.

"Well, I hope so," she replied.

"Sometimes doctors aren't as straitlaced as we think they are," William commented.

Then he asked Miss Worthley where Rowena's brownstone was on Commonwealth Avenue, because he wanted to see the star magnolia if he happened to be in Boston. She explained that it was almost directly across from the statue of General Glover, a Revolutionary War hero from Marblehead, but that now it was May and the tree was no longer in bloom.

But there are other signs of spring, she said. The next item on her nature calendar was the arrival of the bobolinks. "They spend a day or two in the meadow behind my field as they migrate northward. I could die happy just listening to them."

"You get more out of life than anyone I've ever met," William told Miss Worthley.

"I'm just a self-centered old woman who does whatever she wants to do, whenever she chooses to do it," she replied sternly.

"Not in my book. I happen to love you like a member of my own family."

"William," she said, "stop talking like that. You're bringing tears to my eyes."

How the subject of the escalating Vietnam War came up, neither could recall. To William it was an ever-present worry; he knew that eventually he would hear from his draft board, as had several other young people in his company. As far as he knew, he was in good physical condition except for a minor knee problem aggravated while playing football in high school. He felt that if he was called upon, he should serve his country.

The revelation struck horror in Miss Worthley's heart; it brought back memories of her own tragedy almost fifty years before. All she could manage to say before hanging up the phone was, "Well, I certainly hope you won't have to go."

While cleaning the sun porch a couple of days later in preparation for Rowena and Charles's visit, Miss Worthley had a twinge of pain in her chest. Without a moment's hesitation she took a nitroglycerin tablet. The pain went away, but for the rest of the day she paced herself carefully.

Later that day she called Lester Baldwin to order the items she needed for Sunday's tea.

"Lester," she said, "I'm leaving everything up to you as far as the vegetable selection goes. I don't have the time or the energy to get over there."

He told her not to worry about a thing.

Late the following Saturday afternoon, Lester delivered

her order himself, even adding some extras, including a box of brightly colored toothpicks and a modest bouquet of cut flowers, at no extra charge. He was quick to tell her one more time that he had kicked the toothpick habit, and the box of colored toothpicks was to remind her of that.

As he removed each vegetable from the box, he eulogized its freshness, quality, and perfection. His little ceremony almost drove her mad.

Out of politeness she asked him to stay a few minutes for a cup of tea, but he said he had one more stop to make. Just as he reached the door, he turned and said he'd heard from a reliable source that May had been inquiring about her nephew, William.

"Good night, Lester," she said, giving him the cold Worthley stare, "and thanks for the flowers and the toothpicks."

*A*ll the cucumber and deviled ham sandwiches were made by eleven o'clock Sunday morning. For dessert Miss Worthley had painstakingly put together a strawberry parfait. She didn't want Rowena to think she was skimping on anything.

Charles and Rowena arrived at two o'clock. Charles was tall and distinguished looking, with clear blue eyes and silver gray hair. He had a delightful smile.

Miss Worthley gave them the grand tour of the property. By the time they reached the gazebo, Charles was quite impressed by her knowledge of the local flora and fauna and seemed fascinated by her dissertation on alewives. Unfortunately, it was almost low tide in Staddleford Creek, so he was unable to actually see the alewives swimming upstream.

"Charles knows I can't tell a pine tree from a dandelion," Rowena said, "but I've managed to keep that star magnolia alive all these years."

"That's because you never touched it," Charles teased laughingly.

"Charles!" Rowena exclaimed.

"My apologies, Rowena. Just interjecting a little humor into the outing."

Charles was quite taken by Miss Worthley, and because he was an outdoorsman he seemed to have much in common with her. At least twice Rowena interrupted their conversation to let them know she was there.

As Miss Worthley was pouring tea, Charles asked, "Do you have a given name, or is 'Miss Worthley' part of your mystique?"

She was speechless for a moment and tried to disregard his question.

"Well," said Charles, "I'm waiting."

"I do have a given name," she replied unflinchingly, "but I'm not telling you what it is. Now, where were we?"

"We were trying to find out your given name," he said, not about to drop the subject.

"Rowena, dear," Miss Worthley said, "will you please walk out to the kitchen, get a large glass of water, and pour it all over this man's head?"

They all laughed, then Rowena said, "Charles, I think you'd better drop the subject. My cousin is quite touchy about it."

"There are ways to find out what it is," he threatened.

"And if you do, and address me by it, I shall forever put the Worthley curse upon your soul," she said with a smile but also with a look reserved for just this kind of situation.

"Very well," Charles replied. "From this moment on, I shall forever refer to you as the Lady Worthley."

While they were having tea, Charles noticed the old phonograph on the table in the corner of the room. After excusing himself to stretch his legs, he walked over to examine it.

Miss Worthley apologized that the record on it was the only one she had, and it was badly scratched. He recognized the label and said it was a lovely old song. He asked if she would play it for him.

No one would have been the wiser if she had simply said that the phonograph didn't work. Instead, she walked over to the phonograph and carefully placed the stylus on the record.

"The song is from World War I, right?" said Charles, after hearing a few bars.

"Yes," she replied softly, the nostalgia already getting the best of her.

"Rowena," Charles said, "is it all right with you if the Lady Worthley takes a few steps around the room with me?"

Before Rowena could answer, Charles took Miss Worthley's hand, placed his other hand on the small of her back, and guided her onto the sun porch.

She didn't resist, and for about ninety seconds they danced as the music from the scratchy old record floated outside and was carried away by a soft May breeze. For a few of those moments the words to the song flashed through her mind.

> *Poor Butterfly! 'neath the blossoms waiting—*
> *Poor Butterfly! For she loved him so.*
> *The moments pass into hours,*
> *The hours pass into years,*
> *And as she smiles through her tears,*
> *She murmurs low,*
> *The moon and I,*
> *Know that he be faithful,*
> *I'm sure he come to me bye and bye,*
> *But if he don't come back,*
> *Then . . .*

Miss Worthley broke away from Charles and turned off the phonograph.

"Wait a minute," Charles exclaimed, "I want to have a dance with Rowena!"

"Charles, you know I'm not much of a dancer," she said. "Here, let me pour you another cup of tea. It's a long ride home, and I want you to be alert."

"I have to do what the chief surgeon tells me," he replied, looking at Miss Worthley.

"We hate to leave you with this mess of dishes," said Rowena. "Let me help you clean up."

"No . . . no . . . This won't take me long," Miss Worthley replied. "Another time we'll have dinner, and then you both can help. Right, Charles?"

"Absolutely right, Lady Worthley. And I'll wash, because I'm an experienced scrubber," he answered, smiling.

Just before they left, Miss Worthley took them to the carriage house and showed them the phoebe nest, which now held five eggs.

"She's been here for so many years, I'm going to start charging her rent," Miss Worthley said, laughing.

The two cousins hugged each other, then Charles leaned over and kissed Miss Worthley on the cheek. "Well, we're practically family now," he said. "Thank you for the lovely afternoon, and we'll see you at the wedding."

"It was nice to meet you, Charles, and I'm sorry I danced so stiffly, but it's been years . . ."

"No apologies necessary. I'm no Fred Astaire myself, m'lady."

As soon as they left, Miss Worthley carried all the dishes into the kitchen. Then she returned to the library and sank onto the sofa. The dishes could wait until morning. Sometime during the long twilight she got up from the sofa, turned on a light in the kitchen, and closed the windows on the sun porch. She was in bed by nine.

In the meadow behind the field, the bobolinks had arrived when she and Charles were dancing, but their cheerful calls had been blown away from the house by the breeze. Flint heard their song as soon as he arrived in the morning. He told Miss Worthley, and she stood near the sassafras clump for hours, watching the bobolinks through her binoculars.

She didn't get to the dishes until noon, and by then the strawberries, sugar, egg whites, and cream had hardened to the consistency of cement on the parfait glasses. She vowed never to let the dishes wait again. As she scrubbed them, she whistled incessantly in an attempt to imitate the "Roberts," her term for the bobolinks.

Three days before the wedding, Miss Worthley had her worst angina attack yet. It was brought on by her going down into the creek at low tide on a trash collecting expedition. Slogging through the mud and gathering many pounds of debris by herself left her completely exhausted. When she climbed back up the bank, she could hardly breathe. By the time she reached the house, the pain in her chest was so excruciating that she thought she was going to die. Again, the tablets proved their worth, but it took two days of doing nothing before she started to feel strong again.

The wedding was at two o'clock in the afternoon, which gave Miss Worthley plenty of time to get to Boston and over to Brookline without rushing.

The ceremony was brief. Charles had instructed his son Todd to drive Miss Worthley from the church to the reception. In spite of her pretty lavender dress, she looked wan and every bit her age. As Charles was introducing Todd to Miss Worthley a few minutes after the ceremony, he noticed how pale she looked and asked her how she'd been feeling.

"It's not your worry, Charles," she replied, "but I had a dreadful angina attack a few days ago."

"Who's your physician?" he asked.

"A Doctor Sutherland. Her office is a few doors from Rowena's house," she replied.

"Well," he said, "you couldn't be in better hands, from what I've heard about her. Have you talked to her since this last attack?"

"No," she replied.

"Give her a call," he suggested. "You're her patient. It'll give you peace of mind just to talk to her."

She told Charles she would, and thanked him for his concern. He kissed her on the cheek and called her "my new cousin-in-law."

When Miss Worthley arrived at the reception, she felt out of place and wished more people were there so she wouldn't be so conspicuous. However, Todd had been delegated to keep an eye on her, and he made her feel quite at home. She even began to enjoy herself. The champagne toast, which she downed in one swallow on an empty stomach, further relaxed her, and she lost track of how much white wine she drank at the buffet.

Charles's family was delightful, especially Todd, who reminded her of William. After the reception Todd drove her to North Station and waited with her until she boarded the train.

As Flint drove her home from Staddleford Depot, she told him she was tired, "but it's a nice kind of tiredness." She said she'd had a lovely day. "Charles's son Todd waited on me as if I were the Queen of Sheba. I do wish I could have spent more time with Rowena. I'm her only cousin, but she was meeting most of Charles's family for the first time."

"It's kinda nice they had someone lookin' after you," Flint commented, "but it sounds like they had you outnumbered twenty to one, ma'am."

Miss Worthley laughed. "That's just about what it was, too." She paused. "Do you know, Flint, I had more wine today than I've had in the last ten years. I know I was a little tipsy for a while. Drank a whole glass of champagne in one gulp before I had any food in my stomach. Then I had at least two more glasses of white wine after that. Charles told me that drinking an occasional glass of wine would be good for me. I'm glad there wasn't any dancing, because I'd have made a fool of myself. The funny thing was, though, I actually started to feel like dancing."

"But you wouldn't have danced, ma'am," Flint said. "Not if you were feelin' a little tipsy. You wouldn't a let yourself go that much. You're too proper. But," he added, "a drink now and then won't do you much harm. I had a couple a beers this afternoon while I was out fishin'. Helps take the edge off sometimes."

He was quiet for a moment. "You got any wine in the house, ma'am?"

"No, I don't think so, Flint."

"Tell you what," he said. "Next week I'm bringin' you a bottle of good white wine." He paused a moment. "Nope. Make that two bottles. I'll get it in Newburyport where they don't know me, or you, too well. Can't have the tongues waggin'. If I bought a bottle of wine at Lester's, he'd blabber it all over town before I got back here with it. He knows I don't drink wine."

She laughed. "Flint, if you bring it, I'll drink it, but not all in one day. Just enough to 'take the edge off,' as you say."

As she got out of the car in front of the house, Flint said, "Miss Worthley, I think goin' to that weddin' today was one of the best things that's happened to you in a long time."

He had stepped out of the car and was standing next to her in the driveway. She looked at him, his rugged face plainly visible in the light cast by the moon. "So do I, Flint. So do I."

"Miss Worthley," he said, "I really like that dress you're wearin'. And ya know what?"

"What, Flint?"

"The moon gives it kind of a special glow."

"Really, Flint? Must be something in the material."

"Must be," he acknowledged.

"Good night, Flint."

" 'Night, ma'am. Be over on Monday."

Somewhere off in the woods an owl hooted. In the small pond at the edge of the meadow a bullfrog croaked. But for those sounds there was silence, the silence that takes place on a warm June evening when everything seems perfect.

Miss Worthley didn't feel well the next morning.
A letdown, she told herself. Natural after having a good
time. Can't have a hangover from that amount of wine. Not
sick . . . not tired. Weak would describe it. Almost like the
way I felt after the last angina attack. Coming down with a
cold? Don't have any cold symptoms. I'll wait another day,
then call Doctor Sutherland. It's Sunday anyway. I wish Flint
was around so I could talk to him. It would take my mind off
myself. But I'll probably feel better tomorrow.

It was an effort for Miss Worthley to walk up the stairs to
her bedroom. So she decided to nap on the sofa in the library. After all, that was the napping place. Trouble was, she
felt that she could sleep all day. She drank two cups of coffee
to pep her up. It did for a while, but she was ready for bed
by six o'clock. She stretched out on the terrace chaise until
the mosquitoes drove her into the house. From the sun
porch she looked toward the gazebo and decided she didn't
have the strength to walk down to it.

She loved this time of day. The salt marsh looked like
green velvet. She watched the tree swallows as they swooped
gracefully about the yard and gorged themselves on mosquitoes. She could see the two beehives, which Flint had traded

for a few bales of salt-marsh hay, on the stone wall at the edge of the field. The buckwheat that Flint had planted in the field would be in blossom soon, and Miss Worthley looked forward to hearing the drone of bees on warm days as they pollinated the buckwheat blossoms. In fall, Flint would collect the honey from the hives. Buckwheat honey wasn't the best, but it was good enough to put on pancakes and waffles now and then.

At half past six William telephoned from New Haven. As soon as Miss Worthley heard his voice, she felt much better. He was calling from the home of Patricia's parents, where he'd been invited to spend the weekend. He wanted a report on the wedding.

She told him that she'd had a wonderful day, that Charles's family had been more than kind to her, and that she had drunk too much wine.

William laughed. "That's what happens when the country girl goes to the big city."

"I just wish there had been dancing, although I was probably too tipsy to dance," she told William.

"There'll be dancing at my wedding, and you'll be there," he said. "We'll be formally engaged as soon as Patricia selects the ring, but I'd like to give her the cameo right away, if that's all right with you."

"I should say no, but you seem to get the best of me all the time, so I'll make an exception. Give it to her with all my love," she replied.

For a few minutes after she hung up, she felt better, but by half past seven she was so weak that she could hardly walk upstairs to her bedroom. That night she slept almost twelve hours, which meant she missed the sunrise, something she hadn't done more than a handful of times over the years.

But she was hungry when she awoke, and she ate a good breakfast.

At nine o'clock she called Doctor Sutherland. Even though the doctor had examined Miss Worthley only once and had talked to her on the phone just two or three times, she had developed a fondness for her. Because of this, she had neither the heart nor the courage to tell her the truth about her health—that in all probability she would be an invalid by summer's end.

Instead, she told Miss Worthley that she would have good days and bad days, which was true for the time being. On good days she'd feel as though she could walk to Newburyport; on bad days she'd hardly make it out of bed in the morning.

"Are you saying in double-talk that I'm dying?" Miss Worthley asked.

Doctor Sutherland hesitated a moment before she replied. "Not really, but—"

"But what?" Miss Worthley demanded.

"What I'm telling you is that, with your heart, anything can happen. You should curtail just about all your physical activities. Take very short walks. Sleep downstairs so you won't be climbing up and down except on rare occasions. And if you must go upstairs, do it slowly."

Her heart was pounding as Doctor Sutherland spoke. "I never went up a flight of stairs slowly in my life." She felt desperate, but she tried to be calm. "I have no other choice but to try and be a good patient," she said finally.

With Doctor Sutherland's words still ringing in her ears, Miss Worthley picked up the telephone again. A good verbal battle in the morning with someone she didn't like would take her mind off her worries. She called her lawyer, C. J. Whittaker, whose office at the corner of Beacon and Tremont Streets in Boston looked out over the Old Granary Burial Ground. Although the law firm he represented had been handling the Worthley's legal affairs since the turn of the century, Miss Worthley's father had always been suspicious of him. Miss Worthley, who inherited her father's distrust, referred to C. J. as a "wizened old reprobate," in reference to his many supposedly shady dealings involving some members of the General Court. She always thought of him as a chicken without any meat on it, dressed in a dark pinstriped suit.

C. J. was looking out his office window across the old cemetery toward the Park Street Church, a view he cherished. He stood tall and straight, as tall and straight as any man five feet five inches tall with shoes on could stand.

He shuddered when his secretary told him that Miss Worthley was on the phone.

When she told him that she wanted to make some changes to her will, he immediately balked.

"You don't even know what they are yet, and you're already trying to talk me out of them," she snapped.

He told her to think over her request, then come into his office on Thursday and discuss the proposed changes in person.

"I'll do nothing of the sort!" she exclaimed. "You'll come to Staddleford as soon as your little feet can get you out here, or else I shall engage the services of another attorney. Now when can I expect to see you?" she demanded.

There was a pause, then C. J. said, "I guess I can make it Thursday." He knew that it was pure folly to try to delay the trip. "How about one-thirty?"

"One-thirty will be fine," she replied. "These are major changes, C. J., so bring a sharp pencil."

After Miss Worthley hung up, she went out to the terrace, took a deep breath, and filled the birdbath. It was ten o'clock by the gnomon's shadow, which on a sunny day always showed the correct time. Feeling stronger, she headed down to the gazebo. She wanted her walking stick, which was

hanging on a nail inside the door. A year ago Flint had made
the stick for her from a slender birch branch he had pulled
out of an abandoned beaver lodge. He drilled a hole in the
stick and slipped a leather thong through it to fit over her
wrist. Although she had used it once when she inspected the
creek at low tide, relying on a walking stick was not part of
the Worthley tradition. Neither her father nor her mother
had ever used one.

She took down the walking stick from the nail and looked
it over. Still visible on one end was a thin strip of white bark
the beaver had missed. The teeth marks on the stick gave it
character, she thought. She leaned on it. "My new third leg,"
she said aloud, then hobbled back to the house.

On Thursday she was awake long before dawn, lying in bed
meditating on the changes she would make in her will. At
the first hint of daylight she was out of bed. With the sunrise
and the morning's first breeze, the ground fog dissipated
from the marsh. It would be a warm day.

When C. J. arrived she didn't offer him so much as a glass
of water. She had written every one of the changes to her will
on a sheet of paper and simply handed it to him.

He winced as he read them. In the old will, everything,
including the house and land, would have gone to Rowena.
C. J. knew that as soon as Miss Worthley died and the will was
probated, Rowena would probably sell the property. He had
a buyer waiting in the wings who envisioned putting up several houses on the land. Miss Worthley's property was one of
the few buildable parcels in Staddleford because of all the
wetlands in the town. She had been approached by many
speculators who wanted to purchase this prime multi-acre
building site.

Miss Worthley told C. J. to prepare a new will with all the

changes and mail it to her. After she signed it, she would have it notarized in Newburyport and send it back to him. "Better yet," she said, "make two copies. I'll keep one in my safe-deposit box in the bank in Newburyport."

C. J. Whittaker had a bad headache when he left Staddle-ford on that warm June afternoon.

*A*round four o'clock that afternoon, Flint knocked at the kitchen door. He was carrying a large paper bag.

"Got that wine, ma'am," he said as Miss Worthley opened the door. "It's cold, too. Just picked it up in Newburyport. Don't suppose you'd like to sample it, bein' as hot as it is."

"Flint," she said, "you came just at the right time, because I feel like celebrating. Let me get the corkscrew."

"If it's okay by you, Miss Worthley," Flint said, "I'm about to have a swallow of this beer before I leave." He pulled a quart bottle out of the bag.

"It's all right with me, Flint," she said. "Let's go sit on the terrace. The sun should be off it by now. You go sit out there. I'll get the corkscrew and the glasses. Don't you dare drop that firewater," she added, giggling.

She came outside a few minutes later with the corkscrew and a plate full of crackers and cheese. After a struggle, Flint popped the wine cork.

"Now, don't drink that too fast, ma'am," he cautioned as he filled her glass. "On a hot day like this, wine can really creep up on you, give you an awful wallop."

"I'll drink it slowly, Flint," she said. "After the experience I had at Rowena's wedding, I'll be extracautious."

"That's one of the reasons I stick with beer, ma'am. Doesn't usually bother a person the way wine does," he said.

"I never had a glass of beer in my life, Flint."

"Glass a beer now and then's good for the system, ma'am," he said as he poured himself a glass. " 'Course it doesn't taste like the beer they made when I was a young fella. There was a beer I drank then, was black as ink. Phew!" he exclaimed. "Coupla glasses of that stuff and . . . Well, you didn't know what day it was after a little while."

"Oh, Flint," she said, and laughed.

"How's that wine taste, ma'am?"

"It's delicious, Flint. Have some crackers and cheese with your beer," she said as she passed him the plate.

"Thanks, ma'am, I am kinda hungry. Usually on a hot day like this I'm thirsty as a racehorse, but today I'm hungry *and* thirsty."

For a few moments they were both silent.

"Flint," Miss Worthley said, "do you eat all your meals at home, or do you go out now and then?"

"Funny you should ask that, ma'am," he replied. "There's an air-conditioned diner down near the Ipswich line that has a 'special' on Thursdays. Thinkin' a goin' down there tonight. Usually, though, I rustle up somethin' m'self down at the house."

Flint drank some more beer and placed the glass on the table. Then, looking at her, he said, "You like to go down there with me tonight, ma'am? My treat. Special's a boiled dinner, but you don't have to have that. Lots of other things on the menu. All home-cooked food. Run by nice people. I been goin' down there for years. Can't beat the apple pie. Give you a second cup of coffee and don't even charge you for it."

"It sounds wonderful, Flint, but I'm rather tired. It's been an exhausting day for me. I was awake long before dawn. Made some changes to my will. That man you saw leaving earlier is my attorney. He wasn't too happy about what I wanted to do."

100

She paused, then said, "Flint, you won't be offended if I don't go with you tonight, will you?"

"Oh, no, ma'am. We can go another time." He picked up the glass of beer. "And it doesn't have to be on a Thursday, either."

Miss Worthley sipped her wine, and Flint took a cracker and bit into it. They were looking at each other.

"Flint, have you by any chance noticed lately that I haven't been as active as I once was?"

"Now that you mention it, ma'am, I guess I have. Somethin' wrong?"

"Yes, Flint, there is. That angina I told you I have . . . Well, my heart's not what it used to be. I just haven't felt as strong as I once felt. There have been days when I didn't have the strength to walk down to the gazebo. Can you imagine me not walking down there at least once or twice a day in good weather?"

"No, ma'am, I can't."

"Well, Flint, I don't want to alarm you, but . . . I really think I'm dying."

"What do you mean, you think you're dyin'?"

"Just what I said. When I asked my doctor on Monday if I was dying, she gave me some medical double-talk. Oh, she meant well, but I know she was just being kind to me. She told me to move downstairs. Take little walks. Walk slowly. Take naps. Don't rush. Do this. Don't do that. In other words, Flint, she as much as told me to stop living. That's the same thing as telling me I'm dying."

Flint sat in stunned silence. Then he stood up, stared at her, and looked toward the gazebo. "Excuse me, ma'am," he said softly. "I'm goin' down by the creek. Be back in a couple a minutes. Don't you go away, now."

"I'll be right here when you come back." She watched him until he disappeared behind the red cedars.

At that moment the water in Staddleford Creek was quietly returning to the ocean with the outgoing tide. There was still enough water in the creek so that Flint was able to lean over and splash some of it on his face and the back of his neck. He stood up, leaned over again, and splashed more water on his face, this time with his mouth open. He tasted the brine as if it held some elixir that would erase Miss Worthley's words, which were still racing through his mind.

When he came back to the terrace, the first thing he did was move his chair closer to hers. Then he sat down. He was quiet, almost sulking.

"Are you all right, Flint?" she asked.

He didn't say anything.

"Flint!" she exclaimed. "I'm going to need you more now than I ever did."

He finally looked up at her. "That goes without sayin', ma'am. You just tell me the things you want me to do, and then consider them done."

"Oh, Flint," she said, "you don't know what that means to me."

Neither of them spoke for a moment or two. A breeze sighed through the tops of the pine trees.

"Flint," Miss Worthley said, "I know this isn't the best time to ask you this, but I was wondering if you'd consider moving into the carriage house for a while. The two rooms are in good condition, the shower works, and there's always plenty of hot water. The only thing that's missing is a refrigerator in the kitchenette. I can buy one that would fit right into that empty space across from the stove. I hate to even suggest it, but the way I've been feeling the last few days, and after talking to Doctor Sutherland this morning, well, it's . . . I . . . Flint . . . You don't have to tell me right away . . . Oh, dear." She stopped talking and her eyes filled with tears.

Flint drank the rest of his beer in one swallow and leaned back in his chair. "Miss Worthley, I been here almost seventeen years now. After I was here about a month, I said to my-

102

self, 'Flint Fletcher, you're a lucky fella to be workin' here. This lady's somethin' special.'

"Ma'am," he said, "I'll be all moved in there this weekend. And don't you worry 'bout that refrigerator. Barney Little owes me a favor. I'll have him help me move mine over here in his pickup, along with a few other things, includin' my bed, of course."

"Flint, I don't know what to say." The tears streamed down her face as she said it.

"You don't have to say anything, ma'am. Hate to see you cryin' though. If you don't stop, you'll have me doin' the same thing, and I haven't cried since I was a little kid when my mother died."

Miss Worthley wiped away the tears with a napkin, apologizing to Flint as she did it. "The Worthleys aren't supposed to show any emotion. That's what my father always told me. When my mother died, my father never displayed the slightest hint of sorrow. All he said was, 'Life goes on, child. Your mother was a good woman. If you follow in her footsteps, you'll have nothing to be ashamed of in this world.' He said this as if he was reading it from a newspaper. The strange thing was that I wasn't a child. I was thirty-four. This must have been a little token of the paternal feeling he had for me.

"When he died, I never shed a tear, not because I didn't love him, but because it had been drilled into me all my life that Worthleys are disciplined. He was that way in his business dealings. I know he made a lot of enemies in his lifetime. Rowena told me things about him that I never knew. She wasn't being malicious, but he was not a popular man. He had no use for Catholics. Once, one of his partners hired a young man who was Catholic. My father was so mad that he talked about it for weeks.

"You know, Flint," she admitted, "I've been the same way, thanks to him. To think that, because William's last name is Ryan, I supposed he was Catholic when he introduced himself for the first time. I could have cut out my tongue as soon as I said it. I'm glad I apologized to him."

Flint, a little embarrassed by Miss Worthley's personal revelations, shuffled his feet. "I was baptized a Catholic, ma'am. Think it was the last time I was ever in a Catholic church. I guess most of us are all mixed up when it comes to religion."

They were silent again. The woodnotes of a dozen different songbirds were serenading the afternoon.

"Does Bill know how you been feelin', ma'am?"

"No, Flint. Not the way I've felt for the last few days, but he is aware of my heart condition. If it wasn't for his recommending Doctor Sutherland and having me promise to go to her, I'd probably be dead by now."

"He's a nice young fella. Never did get him down into the creek at low tide this spring, did we? Had the Wellingtons all cleaned up for him to wear if we did."

"No, we didn't, and I'm in no condition to do it now. We probably never will. He's moving to New Haven this fall. I'll be lucky to see him again after that. He may have to go into the army.

"Flint, if anything happens to me, I want you to keep in touch with him. I have his telephone number and address. You must remind me to give them to you."

"Yes, ma'am, but I wish you wouldn't talk like that. You got to lick this thing an' go on livin' the way you always did."

"I'm doing my best, Flint, but I think I'm losing the battle. Right now, I don't think I could walk upstairs to my bedroom, and there's something up there I want to show you. Flint, would you mind getting something from my bedroom? On my not too tidy dresser there's a photograph of a soldier. I'd appreciate it if you'd bring it downstairs and put it on the coffee table in the library. And don't you dare cast your eyes on my unmade bed," she said, laughing.

Flint returned to the terrace in short order.

"None of my business, ma'am," he said, "but the fella in

104

that picture looks enough like Bill Ryan to be his twin brother."

"They do look alike, don't they? But it's just a coincidence, Flint."

He looked at Miss Worthley as if to ask, is that all there is to say about it?

"The soldier in that picture was killed in action at the end of World War I," said Miss Worthley. "We were to be married as soon as the war ended."

She sighed. "I guess it was the heartbreak of my life. . . . But I'm alive and he died when he was only twenty-five, so I'm being selfish talking this way."

"Guess we've all had some heartbreak in our lives, ma'am," said Flint. "Had my share, but it's all water over the dam for me. Think if I had my life to live all over again, I wouldn't change a thing."

"You're much more philosophical than I ever imagined, Flint."

"Don't know what you'd call it, ma'am, but I'm contented doin' just what I been doin' all these years, 'specially since I came here."

"Flint Fletcher! You just paid me a wonderful compliment."

"Don't mention it, ma'am. Just tellin' you the truth."

"Flint, you're absolutely one in a million."

"Givin' it to you straight from the shoulder, ma'am, the way I would to anyone else I liked. Wouldn't a stayed here if I didn't feel that way."

She leaned over and grasped one of Flint's large hands with both of hers. "What would I ever have done without you all these years? And now you're still here, and you'll be here almost night and day if I should ever need you in an emergency."

Then, still holding his hand, she said, "You know, Flint, I worry that something will happen to William if he goes into the army, with the way the war has been escalating lately. To think I've known him only since late February and he's affected my life so much. I made a vow early in the morning of the first day he came here, and it's changed my whole outlook on life. Anyone would think that at this point in life, a person wouldn't change, but I have. Look at the reputation I had and probably still have among some of the townspeople. They call me 'Sneakers' Worthley, alewife watcher and bird-watcher, and a crabby, cynical old lady. I call myself 'Worthless' Worthley, a nickname some of my father's employees gave him."

She released her grip on Flint's hand and caught her breath for a moment. "That Saturday morning when you and I went into May's for coffee, wasn't that an eye-opener for a little cross section of Staddleford?"

She didn't wait for him to answer. "No, Flint, I really love them all. I didn't before, but I do now. Or maybe I did all along and didn't realize it until now. Those people have all been a good part of my life for almost fifty years. Oh, I used to think I was a proper Bostonian. Still do, once in a while, but now I consider myself a 'townie.' "

"In my book you're a coupla notches above a townie, ma'am."

"Not really, Flint. Not really."

He shuffled his feet, leaned over, and scratched his ankle.

"I should head down to the diner pretty soon. Hafta get cleaned up a little. Anything you want me to do before I leave?"

"No, Flint. I think I can handle everything for now." She went to pick up the tray.

"Here, ma'am, I'll carry that for you. You just sit there and take it easy, though you won't be able to sit there much longer 'cause the mosquitoes'll be after you b'fore you know it. Only thing's keepin' them away now's that little breeze that keeps comin' up every so often."

"Then I think I'll go in with you right now, Flint."

He placed the tray next to the kitchen sink. "Ma'am, I'm an expert dishwasher. Only take a minute ta give these things a quick rinse."

"No, Flint, you just leave them right there. I'll get to them in due time. You go now and enjoy your supper."

"Okay, ma'am. See you tomorrow. You call if you need me. Should be home around nine."

*I*t took more than one sunny day for the heat to get inside the big old house. Miss Worthley draped her new pale blue cardigan over her shoulders, sat down on the sofa, and was glancing at Warren's photograph when the telephone rang. It was Rowena, just back from their wedding trip. Bubbling with her usual vocal energy, she talked nonstop about their honeymoon. The last thing she said before she hung up was that it was a good thing she wasn't of childbearing age, for she definitely would be pregnant by now.

Rowena hadn't even asked her how she was feeling. Oh, well, thought Miss Worthley, I can forgive her. She's still all wrapped up in connubial bliss. Miss Worthley laughed out loud as the phrase went through her mind. Then she realized she hadn't told Rowena that Flint would be moving into the carriage house this weekend. That would have given her something to talk about with Charles. I guess we're even, she thought to herself.

As she rested on the sofa, she got a second wind. The thought of having Flint nearby most of the time gave her a feeling of well-being.

"It was nice to hear from Rowena," she mused aloud. "I never had a chance to ask for Charles. I'll call in a few days and perhaps he'll answer the telephone. If not I'll ask to speak to him, thank him for having Todd as my guardian angel on their wedding day."

She liked Charles. There was a certain mysterious air about him, she decided. Leave it to Rowena to find someone as nice as he is, she thought with a sigh. I spent my whole life feeling sorry for myself after Warren was killed.

She sighed again. "Flint is right," she said aloud. "It's all water over the dam. What would I ever do without that man? He's the one person in this world I can really depend on, and he's been right here with me all these years."

She walked to the kitchen to make her dinner; tonight, she decided, it would be just a sandwich and a cup of tea. Then she washed the dishes. Feeling stronger, she decided that she would sleep in her bedroom tonight. She wanted to greet tomorrow's sunrise from the upstairs windows.

In the middle of the marsh, heat waves produced by the sun danced above the surface of the water. It was so warm that even the birds were quiet. But in the higher air a slight breeze stirred and made sitting on the terrace tolerable.

As Miss Worthley reclined on the chaise, she heard a car door slam. A few moments later Flint led William onto the terrace.

"Look who the cat dragged in, ma'am," Flint said.

"William!" she exclaimed. "Oh, but I should have been expecting you. It's Friday."

He leaned over and kissed her on the forehead.

"Flint, do you see how this Beau Brummell takes advantage of me?"

"Probably no more dangerous than I am, ma'am."

"But at least I've known you for a long time, Flint." They all laughed, then Flint started to walk away.

"Don't you dare leave, Flint. I want you and William right

110

here. It's seldom that I have two handsome men standing over me. Sit down, sit down, both of you."

"Flint told me he's moving into the carriage house this weekend," William said after they were seated.

"That's right. I'm supposed to take it easy—Doctor Sutherland's orders. I'm fine today, but I'm not about to walk into Staddleford Center. I've been down to the gazebo once, so that takes care of today's walk. I'm not even making you a cup of tea."

"I don't need a thing," William said. "I'll stop at May's later on."

"You wouldn't dare. You're teasing me, you brute!"

"Yes, I am, and I apologize," William said, smiling.

"Apology accepted. Now, what do you have to report?" she asked as if she was the chairman of the board.

"Well, Patricia sends her love." He was pensive for a moment. "The bad news is I'll be getting my draft notice any day now."

Her face clouded. "Oh, dear, I was afraid of that."

"I don't think it will happen until after I move to New Haven. It seems inevitable, but at this point I just want to get it over with."

Flint interrupted. "I've got a big thermos full of ice-cold lemonade. I'll get some glasses and we'll finish it off. Be back in a coupla minutes."

William stayed only long enough to drink a glass of lemonade. He said he was in the process of helping his parents move into their apartment. Although he didn't know it that afternoon, his next visit to Staddleford would not be until September. He shook hands with Flint, then bent to kiss Miss Worthley once more.

Flint was moved into the carriage house by four o'clock Saturday afternoon. Miss Worthley was so grateful that she made up her mind to make another change to her last will.

She called C. J. Whittaker the first thing Monday morning and dictated the change. "Under the category of real estate, I want you to insert the following: Life tenancy is hereby given to Finley Fletcher, a single man, whose address is RFD, Old Haystack Road, Staddleford, Massachusetts, in the premises known as number twenty-five, Staddleford Road, Staddleford, Massachusetts. You can give it the legal phraseology, C. J. Any questions?"

"Yes," he replied tersely. "Who the hell is this Finley Fletcher?"

"He's my gardener and handyman and a very dear and faithful friend," she replied.

"He's not that big oaf who's always standing at the edge of the driveway whenever I go up there, is he?"

"The individual you refer to as 'that big oaf' happens to be the person I care for more than anyone else in the world. Now make the change as quickly as you can, and get the completed will in today's mail, ready for my signature." With a pounding heart, she slammed down the telephone, furious at the despicable man. But at least her affairs were in order.

Barring anything unforeseen, this was the last change she would make to her will. It gave all her real estate to the newly formed Society for the Preservation of the Salt Marsh. A sum of money was to be held in escrow for maintenance and repairs of the main house and the carriage house. Flint would make the minor repairs as long as he was able, and he'd receive a monthly stipend that would be more than adequate even if he lived to be a hundred.

Miss Worthley's books would be donated to the Staddleford Library. A set of encyclopedias, the deluxe edition that William had been trying to sell her, would be purchased and also given to the library. A fund for the maintenance of the Staddleford Parish Church cemetery was to be established in her name. She would be buried there.

As for the house furnishings, Rowena could have whatever she wanted, but Miss Worthley knew there was little chance she'd take anything. Whatever William wanted at a later date, he could have. She would tell Flint to dispose of everything else as he saw fit.

Her jewelry, consisting of a few bracelets and earrings and her mother's solitaire diamond, were Patricia's, if and when she and William married. Otherwise, at the end of ten years, they were to be sold and the money given to the Staddleford Library.

Finally, the Society for the Preservation of the Salt Marsh would maintain the fish ladder at Staddleford Pond in order to perpetuate the alewife run. A sum of money would be set aside for that purpose.

A few days later Miss Worthley received the updated will in the mail, along with C. J.'s bill for professional services. Flint drove her to Newburyport to have the will notarized and copies made. She mailed the original to C. J. but planned to wait a month before she paid his bill.

On the morning of the Fourth of July, Miss Worthley and Flint went into Staddleford to watch the traditional parade, which lasted exactly nine minutes. From the bandstand on Staddleford Green, a perspiring Reverend Leander Sparks gave a brief discourse on the true spirit of independence and thanked God for giving it to us. Miss Worthley thought he had gained weight since she last saw him on Easter Sunday.

fter the Fourth of July, the summer seemed to fly by. Flint mowed, baled, and stored the salt-marsh hay alone. Even though Miss Worthley's help with these chores in previous summers had been minimal, he felt exhausted by the end of each day. And he missed the companionship she provided.

The buckwheat he had planted in May was in bloom, and the drone of the honeybees as they sweet-talked their way back and forth from the hives to the white-blossomed field seemed to take some of the curse off the sultry days. Flint would often say, "This is growin' weather, and we'll all be lookin' back on days like this next January."

Miss Worthley moved out of her bedroom on August 10; she was no longer able to climb the stairs. She enjoyed sleeping in the library, and the fact that she wasn't running up to her bedroom several times a day seemed to give her new strength. Flint wanted to move her bed downstairs, too, but she said she'd wait until fall. For the time being, the sofa would be her sleeping place.

The sun now rose quite a bit more south of east than it had in late June and early July. The greenhead flies had gone and the salt-marsh mosquitoes seemed less bothersome than they had been a few weeks before. And what started as a once-in-a-while occurrence became a ritual as Flint appeared on the terrace or the sun porch every afternoon to sit with Miss Worthley for a few minutes. Sometimes she'd have made iced tea, or Flint would bring his huge thermos filled with lemonade. A couple of times he surprised her by bringing a bottle of white wine. When he did, he'd also bring a bottle of beer for himself, explaining that he didn't want her drinking alone. She would laugh and ask why he hadn't done it years ago. He'd always say it hadn't been the right time. Then he'd tell her that familiarity breeds contempt, a phrase his mother had used frequently.

William was calling weekly now and one day managed to talk to Flint for a few minutes when Miss Worthley was on the terrace. Flint told him she was doing well, but it was plain that she didn't have much energy. William said he'd be going into the army in mid-September but would visit just before he left and say good-bye to them both. He asked Flint not to tell Miss Worthley that bit of news.

At sunrise on a foggy, misty late-August morning, Miss Worthley walked alone out on the marsh to a tiny island not more than three to four feet higher than the surface of the water. She called the island the "marsh mountain." One scraggly red cedar, a few clumps of bayberry, and a couple of low-bush blueberries were its only vegetation. She always marveled at how the red cedar managed to survive there; its roots tasted brackish water at every flood tide. When Miss Worthley told Flint about her excursion, he scolded her for walking so far.

Just before Labor Day she had a severe angina attack, the worst in weeks. It prompted her to call Doctor Sutherland, who told her to come for another examination, including an EKG the next day. Miss Worthley was reluctant at first but finally agreed.

Knowing how Flint hated to drive in traffic, she decided to take the train. But when it pulled into the depot that morning, Miss Worthley just stood on the platform and made no effort to board.

"What are you waitin' for, ma'am?" said Flint. "Get on!"

"I'm waiting for you to kiss me good-bye, Finley."

The flush on his weathered face was immediately evident. But then he quickly removed his cap, leaned over, and gently kissed her on the forehead.

"That's better," she said. "Now, good-bye, and I'll call from the doctor's office to tell you what train I'm taking back."

"Bye, ma'am. You got your pills?"

"I have. Good-bye again, Flint."

On the ride into Boston, she reviewed everything she had done recently to get her affairs in order. On that account, she was systematic. Housekeeping was another matter altogether.

She started thinking about what would happen after she—after anyone—died. When you were dead, you were dead. That was all there was to it. The living might have some memory of you after you were gone—that is, if there was something to remember you for.

What am I to be remembered for? she wondered. Am I ready to die? No. Not that anyone ever is. I can't even walk as far as the bridge over Staddleford Creek anymore. I can hardly walk to the gazebo. I could try a wheelchair . . . have Flint wheel me down there. No, never!

The shrill whistle of the train momentarily interrupted her thoughts. She started thinking about William and Patricia. She wrote me that lovely note thanking me for the cameo. Will I ever meet her? Probably not. But I can see her right now. I want her to be exactly as my mind sees her. I'm sure the pictures of her that William showed me don't do her justice. I hardly looked at them. They don't show her red hair. She would be beautiful standing on the terrace with William holding her hand, her hair shining in the sunlight. William will come home from the war. Yes, I know he will.

She sighed softly. It would be nice to have Patricia for tea some afternoon. I'd make cucumber sandwiches, the dainty ones, just for her. William can stay out in the carriage house with Flint while Patricia and I have tea alone, the way two women should. That's the proper way to do it.

Her mind rambled on. At times she soliloquized as she stared out the window at the Ipswich marshes. "I have to make sure that Flint keeps mowing all the salt marsh to keep the cattails and phragmites from becoming established. I don't want him using any herbicides, either. I know he won't."

It's almost September, she thought with a sigh. Monarch butterflies will be migrating soon. "Poor Butterfly." I haven't played the record since Charles and Rowena were here that afternoon last spring. Seems so long ago, yet it doesn't. I'll call them from Doctor Sutherland's. I'd love to walk through the Public Garden and take that ride on a swan boat. I don't think I have the strength to walk as far as the swan boats. I never made it to the Pops, either, did I? Oh, dear, where is that fountain of youth? There is no such thing!

I'm glad I went to Rowena's wedding, but I wish Flint had been with me that day. He's not exactly handsome; he's rugged looking. But when he's dressed up, which isn't very often, he looks uncomfortable. Charles is so handsome. Rowena's lucky to have found someone like him, but I couldn't live under the same roof with Charles. But Warren . . . poor Warren. To think I spent all these last years think-ing about him. We almost didn't meet that night at the cotillion. What if we hadn't met? But we did, and I *did* look at him; in fact, I stared at him. He was shy, but he looked at me. Then he walked over and asked me to dance. Three months of the happiest days of my life, his life, our lives. In a sense, I'm a martyr . . . no, Warren's the martyr.

She sighed again.

I'm tired just sitting here on the train. Tired while I'm sitting? That certainly tells me something. I dread the walk

118

to the street to get a cab. I'll walk slowly. I should have let Flint drive me. It would be stressful for him, but he would have, if I'd let him. He's hardly left my side all summer. Oh, dear, it bothers me when I give him his paycheck every week, and I know it bothers him when he accepts it. I'd like to pay him more, but I know he wouldn't accept it, especially now. I'm glad I gave him life tenancy in my will. He loves the place as much as I do, and he'll be sure that the alewives make it into Staddleford Pond every spring. There's no one like Flint, anywhere.

Then she laughed. I know I embarrassed him at the depot. He kissed me as if I had the plague. That's Flint, all right. I must actually love him if I'm thinking about him this way. I believe he really does love me. Oh, it gives me such a good feeling. I'd be dead now if it wasn't for Flint. I know that.

The train was slowing down. "North Station," the conductor called out.

Miss Worthley directed the cabdriver to go around the periphery of both the Common and the Public Garden and to drive slowly so she could see the swan boats.

"You'll never have anyone ask you to drive this slowly again, even if you drive taxis for another twenty years," she told the driver.

"You really like this place, dontcha, lady?"

"It brings back pleasant memories."

"Musta been in love, right?"

"Exactly."

"Thought so. Lotta people fall in love here . . . college kids, all kindsa people. Somethin' about the place, 'specially in spring. Tulips out, all the blossoms, swan boats. Spoiled it, though, when they put that garage under the Common."

He looked at her through the rearview mirror. "S'pose you got a buncha grandchildren."

"No. I never married."

"A nice-lookin' lady like you? Oops, there I go, gettin' personal. My apologies, lady."

"That's all right. Are you married?"

"Sure am. Four boys and a nice wife. I'm a lucky guy. We don't have much, but I manage to put food on the table."

The cab was on Arlington Street, approaching the beginning of Commonwealth Avenue. "What number didja say that was, lady?"

"I don't think I gave you the number, but it's right at the corner of Dartmouth Street and Commonwealth Avenue. A doctor's office," she replied.

They were stopped at a traffic light on Arlington Street. "Nothin' serious, I hope."

"No, no. Just a routine checkup, that's all."

"Good idea to have one every so often. I should have one."

"Yes, you should. You owe it to your family."

"One of these days, I'm gonna."

"Would you mind driving around the Public Garden once more? I'm early for my appointment."

"Don't mind a bit. Ya know, lady, you're good company. I'm shuttin' off the meter right now. Rest of the ride's on me."

"Thank you, but that's really not necessary."

"My pleasure, lady. Lemme see if I can go even a little slower this time."

He drove around once more, then turned onto Commonwealth Avenue and went right past Rowena's. Miss Worthley could see that the star magnolia, green and ordinary looking in late summer, shielded the first-floor windows of the brownstone from the morning sun. She leaned forward, searching for signs of activity, but everything looked as peaceful as the day itself.

"Here we are, lady," the driver said, then he hopped out and assisted her onto the sidewalk.

She handed him a twenty-dollar bill. "That was the loveliest ride I've ever had around here. Thank you very much. You keep all of this."

"Lady, that's a twenty!"

"I know it is, but I like you."

"Thanks a lot, lady, and I hope the doc says you'll live to be a hundred."

"So do I."

Next to the steps leading to Doctor Sutherland's office was a rose of Sharon, its pink blossoms fully open. She lingered for a few moments looking at the lovely bush and wondering if its blooming could be related to the whereabouts of the alewives in late summer. She would try to remember to check her copy of Bigelow and Schroeder when she returned to Staddleford.

For one fleeting moment, as she stood on the sidewalk and looked up and down Commonwealth Avenue, she almost walked away.

Doctor Sutherland gave her a cheerful greeting and shook her hand firmly, then she got right down to business. She asked Miss Worthley if she was ever slow in reaching for the nitroglycerin tablets when she had angina pain. Miss Worthley told her she probably was. The doctor advised speed in this situation, even if Miss Worthley wondered whether the pain was caused by angina or something else. "Better to be safe than sorry" were the doctor's exact words.

While a technician prepared Miss Worthley for the EKG, Doctor Sutherland told her bluntly that people with heart conditions don't get better; they either maintain a status quo or get worse.

"Am I maintaining a status quo?" asked Miss Worthley. Before Doctor Sutherland could reply, she snapped, "No, I'm not. I'm going downhill at a slow trot."

"Please, Miss Worthley, try to be positive. Let's get on with the EKG."

"It's a waste of my time as well as yours. I'm dying, and I don't need this gadget to tell me so."

"Miss Worthley, please!"

When the EKG was completed, Doctor Sutherland studied it for a few moments. "You have a badly damaged heart," she said.

"I know I have a badly damaged heart, or else I wouldn't be here," Miss Worthley countered.

"Let me make a few suggestions," said Doctor Sutherland. "Remain inactive, avoid stress, and try to reduce your intake of fatty foods. Also, be sure to take the nitroglycerine at the *first* hint of chest pain or discomfort."

"You told me all that when I called you in June. You're just using different words today," Miss Worthley said loudly.

"This is exactly the type of situation you should try to avoid," the doctor cautioned.

"Easy for you to say."

"I'm sorry if I seem blunt. I don't mean to be," Doctor Sutherland told her consolingly. She *didn't* tell her that the slightest abnormal situation could cause her heart to fail, and that even if she followed the doctor's orders, she would probably die within a month or two.

Miss Worthley left the office so depressed that she completely forgot to call Rowena or a cab until she reached the sidewalk. As tired and weak as she felt, and as hot and muggy as it was, she managed to walk around the corner and onto Newbury Street, where she called Rowena from a pay phone.

Charles answered. "Where the hell are you?"

"I'm about two blocks away, at the corner of Dartmouth and Newbury Streets."

"Stay where you are. I'll be right over and pick you up. We're going out with friends in about an hour, but I can at least drive you to North Station. Rowena's still getting dressed."

Hearing Charles's voice raised her spirits. She stepped outside the stuffy phone booth and leaned against a tree, which fortunately was in the shade of a building. As inconspicuously as possible, she put her forefinger on her wrist and tried to determine if her pulse was normal. When she couldn't find it, she decided that she was probably dead but didn't know it.

Charles arrived in less than five minutes, kissed her quickly, and helped her into the car. Having already surmised why she was in Boston, he asked if Doctor Sutherland had any encouraging words.

"None whatsoever, Charles. I'm on my way home to die. And please, don't give me any doctor talk."

"I won't. But have you had lunch?"

"Not so much as a glass of water. I forgot all about eating."

"There's a little hole-in-the-wall of a restaurant on Charles Street. We'll stop there and you can have a bite. We have to get you some nourishment for the ride home."

"I have to call Flint and tell him what train I'm taking so he can pick me up at the depot."

Miss Worthley had one brief glimpse of a swan boat as Charles drove past the Public Garden on the way to the restaurant. He called Flint while she was eating and told him what train she'd be on.

At North Station Charles walked her to the train, called her "Cousin No-Name," and kissed her good-bye.

"Charles, you are my savior," she told him. "Thank you so much, and give my love to Rowena."

On a cool, overcast, threatening day in mid-September, William visited Miss Worthley to say good-bye. He would be leaving for army training in a few days.

They sat in the library reminiscing about his first visit and how she'd treated him. They both laughed as they went over all the details again and again. Then they talked about more current matters.

"How do I look, William?" she asked. "Be honest with me, now."

"I've seen you looking better, but maybe it's because I haven't seen you for a while."

"You're being kind to me," she replied.

There was a period of silence, followed by William reminding her that she hadn't bought a set of encyclopedias from him yet.

She told him it would happen in good time, and that she would make sure he received credit for it. He was a little puzzled by her comment but didn't question her further.

Flint surprised them both when he walked in carrying a tray with tea and snacks that he had prepared in the carriage house. Then he excused himself, saying he had to go to Newburyport for a tractor part. A higher-than-normal tide was expected that evening, and he didn't dare leave the tractor on the marsh, where it had stalled while he was cutting the second crop of hay. He wished William good luck and shook his hand.

Miss Worthley and William were quiet for a while, then she asked if he knew the botanical name for salt-marsh grass.

"*Spartina patens,*" he replied.

"William," she said, "you've done your homework well."

There was another period of silence, then William said, "You never played the old phonograph for me."

"I'll play it right now," she said. "Will you dance with me?"

"I will, but I'm supposed to ask you."

"Woman's privilege," she answered. She turned on the phonograph and lowered the stylus to "Poor Butterfly."

William led her to the middle of the library floor. "I don't think I've ever heard this before," he said as they started to dance. "Are there words to it?"

"Yes, but they're sad. I know them as well as my own name. It's an old song that was popular in World War I. I was in love with a young soldier. We danced to it a hundred times. We were going to marry after the war, only he was killed. It was the only romance I ever had, and I never got over it. You . . . you remind me of him. Anyway, my entire outlook in life was affected by that tragedy."

She sighed and continued reminiscing as they danced.

"It was foolish of me to allow myself to mourn—or whatever you want to call it—for fifty years. There aren't many people who know about it. Rowena does, and I'm sure she's told Charles. I told Flint only a few weeks ago. It makes me wish that you and Patricia were getting married right away. No . . . no, I don't, because you'll come home from the war unscathed and you'll marry her."

They danced in silence until the song ended. "That's the only record I own. One scratchy old record. Can you imagine that, William, after all these years? And I love music. Oh, I listen to it on the radio from time to time . . . classical selections, although I do like show tunes. And about every five years I go into Boston to hear the Pops. You'd think I would have bought a few records, wouldn't you? But no, not little old Miss Worthley, the strange one."

The rest of the afternoon was spent in almost as many moments of silence as in periods of conversation. Outside, it had started drizzling.

"Miss Worthley, all good things must come to an end. I have to leave."

She sighed. "Do you remember what I asked you when you were about to leave after your first visit?"

William thought for a moment. " 'Will I ever see you again?' Isn't that what you said?"

"William!" she exclaimed. "You do remember." She paused. "But I won't ask you that now."

She was trying hard to maintain her poise. Holding onto him, just as she had seven months before, they walked down the hallway to the front door.

"I'm not going to linger," said William. "I'm going straight to my car."

"I won't allow you to linger, but do give my love to Patricia."

He kissed her tenderly on the cheek, and she hugged him.

When he was a few feet from his car, she called out, "William, what is good church Latin for 'Peace be with you?'"

He hesitated a moment, turned, and said, "*Pax vobiscum,* Miss Worthley, *pax vobiscum.*"

"I like the sound of it, William. I like the sound of it."

As he reached the car, she called out once more. "*Pax vobiscum,* William, and you be careful driving home in this rain."

He waved and climbed into the car to drive away. It wasn't only the rain that dampened his face.

Miss Worthley placed Warren's photograph back on the coffee table. She had hidden it among the books a few days before, in anticipation of William stopping by.

When Charles and Rowena visited Miss Worthley later in the month, Charles asked if she'd consider going into the hospital for a few days of doing nothing, to see if she might feel stronger after a complete rest.

She told him she wanted to die in her own house and didn't want some nurse waking her up and sticking a thermometer in her mouth every four hours.

"Flint gives me all the care I need," she told them. "He's even washing the dishes now. He doesn't let me do anything anymore. I do the things I shouldn't do only when he goes into Staddleford or over to Newburyport. But he always discovers what I've done and then politely scolds me."

"All the more reason for you to go into the hospital for a while," said Rowena. "Then you won't be able to do *anything*."

"I don't want to *not* do anything. My privacy is something I cherish. Flint knows that. He's the only person in the world who knows when to make an appearance and when not to. That man is there when I want him, and he's not there when I don't want him. I think he's been reading my mind for seventeen years. Many times when I've decided I need him for something, he'll appear almost the moment I've had the thought. He'd make a wonderful butler. Lately, on his own, he brings me tea every afternoon at three-thirty. I think he noticed what time I served tea when William started coming here. He's so observant that he even trims the crusts off the little sandwiches he makes for me. It almost brings tears to my eyes just telling you how kind he's been." She paused. "What time is it, Charles?"

"Almost three-thirty."

"In a couple of minutes," Miss Worthley said, "Flint will walk in here carrying a tray full of goodies and a pot of tea.

I told him only this morning that you were coming, but I said nothing about having tea."

A minute later Flint knocked at the library door, then walked in carrying all the essential ingredients for a proper tea.

A few days after Charles and Rowena visited, Miss Worthley developed a cold and a wracking cough. For almost a week, all she could do was recline on the sofa. Flint's treatment for her malady was a concoction of a double jigger of hundred-proof whiskey and three tablespoons of buckwheat honey, straight from the comb, stirred into a mug of boiling water.

"Don't let it cool off too much before you drink it, ma'am," he advised. "It won't do you any good if it's not hot."

"Why am I letting you force-feed me this . . . this bronchial brew, you witch doctor?" she snapped. "You're trying to cook my esophagus."

In an attempt to cheer her up, Flint jokingly accused her of smoking. He was relieved when she finally rallied from the cold, although her cough persisted.

On the warm October afternoons that followed, she would sit on the terrace, then move to the sun porch when Flint brought her tea about half past three. Her only physical activity was an occasional walk to her perennial garden, where she would cut a few asters.

With each passing day, fall progressed a bit more. Near the pond where the bullfrog had croaked on warm summer evenings, the swamp maples had turned crimson. The sugar maples, green only a few days before, were now pale yellow. The hickories, their leaves drenched in dew and glistening in the early-morning sunshine, were as gold as bullion. The recently emerged alfalfa, which Flint had planted in the field after he harrowed in the buckwheat stubble in September, radiated the verdancy that Miss Worthley now viewed. Beyond the brackish water of the estuary, in pure salt water, the alewives that had hatched in Staddleford Pond in late April and early May were already three to four inches long.

On a cloudless October afternoon, Flint went to Staddleford Center for groceries. Frost had formed in the low spots the previous evening, and the chill in the air warned of a more general freeze that night.

Miss Worthley had waited for Flint's absence to see the sassafras clump in all its autumn beauty. He had barely disappeared when, with her walking stick for support, she hobbled down the path for a glimpse of it. Although the clump was not more than two hundred feet away, she was out of breath when she reached it. She leaned against one of the trees for support, then slowly made her way back to the terrace and stretched out on the chaise, exhausted.

We'll have a hard frost tonight, and that will be the end of the growing season, she said to herself after she caught her breath. I wish William could have seen the sassafras. They're so beautiful, almost orange. And to think the Indians made tea from the twigs. It must have been strong stuff, but I'll stick with the orange pekoe and the oolong.

She was talking out loud now.

"Oo-long, the redwing's song. How does that go? I'll never hear one of those again. . . . I'm awfully cold and tired. I'll pull the throw over my legs. There, that's better. I smell salt-marsh hay. The wind's blowing from the marsh . . . no sweeter smell in the world. . . . I like the long shadows this time of year. I like the smell of burning leaves . . . watching Flint carry in an armful of wood for the fireplace . . . flames reflected off the panes of glass on the French door . . ."

"Oh!" she cried out. "All of a sudden I don't feel good. Flint, are you back? I shouldn't have walked down there. I'm not dying, just tired. Can't be dying. I think I'm ready to die, but not today. God wouldn't let me die on a day this magnificent. Maybe on a rainy day, but not today. Flint, is that you? He should be back by now. I should take one of these pills . . . maybe two. There. . . . But I still don't feel good."

She looked toward the sundial. "Can't tell time any more today. Gnomon's in the shadows."

"Oh!" she gasped. "I feel sick. Flint, is that you? Are you back, Flint? I'll look up at the sky. Think good thoughts. Are those geese up there? I can hear them. Clarion voices calling. Flint? Warren? Poor Warren. Poor Butterfly. Poor Butterfly 'neath the blossoms wait . . . poor butter . . . Flint! Flint!"

Miss Worthley coughed, and coughed again, making a raspy sound that was followed by a long sigh. For an instant, the gurgle of the water in Staddleford Creek seemed louder. A car door slammed. Flint was back. But by now, the geese were only specks in the blue sky.

en years later, on a perfect late-April morning, William Ryan was walking along Commonwealth Avenue. He had found the star magnolia in front of Rowena's brownstone. It seemed more fully blossomed than the other magnolias growing next to the sidewalk.

He crossed Commonwealth Avenue and sat on a bench on the mall directly opposite the white-blossomed magnolia. He reflected on what had happened over the years.

After his discharge from the army, he and Patricia had married. The company sent him to New York and then Chicago, where they were now living. His mother had passed away while he was in Vietnam, and his father died a year later. Patrick, William and Patricia's only child, was born the following year. William hadn't been back to Staddleford until the previous day when they all went there to visit Flint. He and Flint had corresponded and talked on the telephone many times over the years.

Flint told Patricia that anything in the house was theirs. Rowena hadn't taken a thing; she and Charles had moved to Arizona and were living near Charles's youngest son, Todd.

Flint handed Patricia a small jewelry box and told her

she could have whatever she wanted of its contents. She removed a tarnished sterling silver bracelet.

"Strange you should take a fancy to that, ma'am," Flint said. "It was about the only jewelry Miss Worthley ever wore. Wasn't much for wearin' rings and stuff."

"Oh, Flint," she exclaimed. "Leave it to me to find the one thing you remember her wearing most often. I'd feel terrible taking any of these things, to tell you the truth."

"I'm gonna be awful disappointed if you don't take the whole box. Been lookin' forward for a long time to havin' you come up here, meetin' you, and givin' it to you."

Patricia could see by the expression on Flint's face that he meant every word.

"All right, Flint," she replied after a pause. "Thank you. I'll keep them. You're truly everything Bill told me you are." She threw her arms around him and kissed him on the cheek.

Flint blushed. "First time I ever been kissed by a redhead," he said in his own inimitable way.

She laughed. "First time I ever kissed anyone named Flint. Tell me, where did your name originate?"

"Well," he said, still blushing, "I'm supposed to have some Indian blood in my veins, so when I was a kid, I made up the name 'cause I hated my Christian name of Finley. It kinda stuck, and that's the whole story, ma'am."

"Well, I like it. It's very manly," she told him.

Flint was warming up to all of them in good style. He noticed William and Patrick standing off to the side. " 'Bout time we took the little fella for a walk down by the creek so's we can show him some alewives. Tide's just right. You musta done some plannin' to hit it right on the button like this, Bill."

"As a matter of fact, I did. I called an old friend in Boston every other day for two weeks and asked him to drive down Commonwealth Avenue and let me know when he thought

134

the magnolias were close to blossoming. He's convinced I'm crazy. Anyway, Miss Worthley told me that was the way she gauged when the alewives would be coming up Staddleford Creek to spawn."

"She was right, Bill. That's the way she figured it."

Flint looked at Patricia. "You're welcome to come along, ma'am, or if you want, stay here and look over the furniture. Remember now, anything in the house is yours." He hesitated a moment. "Except my bed."

They all laughed.

"Thank you, Flint," she replied. "I think I will stay here and look around. The house is so beautiful, and everything seems so well cared for. It's a pity to even touch anything."

"Reason everything looks so good is that some creepy woman from the salt-marsh crowd comes 'round every week and polishes everything. Got a lot of moxie, that one. Caught her in my bedroom snoopin' one time. Told her it was off-limits and to stay out of it. They're a funny bunch, that marsh crowd. Have meetin's every so often. Invite me once in a while, if they remember. Now they're talkin' about havin' tours here someday. Don't want to be hard to get along with, but I'd just as soon they hold off havin' them till I'm dead. Couldn't stand havin' gangs a people comin' here nosin' around. Don't think Miss Worthley had that in mind, either, when she left it to 'em."

Flint paused. "I s'pose it'll happen someday, but I don't want to be around when it does."

"I hope it doesn't happen for a long time, either, Flint," William said. "I just may write the society a nice friendly little letter on that account. After all," he said, laughing, "Miss Worthley was my great-aunt."

Flint laughed, too, and agreed it wouldn't hurt to write that letter.

"By the way, Flint, whatever became of that old phonograph?" asked William.

Flint seemed surprised that William remembered it. "Oh, I guess it's around here somewhere. Why, did you want it?"

"No, not really," William replied. "I was just curious."

"Well then," Flint said, "let's go see the alewives."

Back on Commonwealth Avenue, William watched as a few of the petals fell from the magnolia and dotted the red-brick sidewalk.

Patricia and Patrick had left the hotel and were walking toward him. He heard Patrick call.

"Dad! Dad! Mom and I thought we lost you."

"No, you didn't," William replied. "I was resting after taking the long way around to go for a ride on the swan boats. Anyone interested in going with me?"

"Yes!" the boy exclaimed.

"Well," William said, "what are we waiting for?"

In Staddleford, everything was finally back to normal. The day before, Patricia had told Flint that it would have been sacrilegious to remove a single item of furniture from the house. As soon as they had left, Flint went out to the carriage house and carried Warren's picture and the old phonograph back to where they had always been kept.

As William and his family were boarding a swan boat in the lagoon of the Public Garden, Flint was standing by the French doors that led to the sun porch. All the windows were open, and the bright April morning sunshine streamed in. He had just placed Miss Worthley's only record on the phonograph.

Helped by a warm breeze, the music from the sentimen-

136

tal old song carried through the tall pines and across the field to the salt marsh. Flint's heart was in tune with everything around him, although his whistle wasn't.

Yes, Flint Fletcher was whistling . . . the same off-pitch, off-key, out-of-tune notes he'd whistled ten Aprils ago when he watched the alewives a few days before Miss Worthley saw them for the last time.